*Thanks to My Husband for
encouraging my creative mind and
amazing support.*

Other Books written by

Joanne Keele

Dreams Collection

Dreams

Author Bio

Joanne Keele has been weaving words into stories since she was a mere child of nine years old, her imagination ignited by the boundless possibilities of storytelling. From those early days filled with whimsical tales and vibrant characters sprung from her youthful mind, she nurtured a passion for writing that quietly simmered beneath the surface for many years. Joanne never took that brave step to put pen to paper for publication, until her First Book Dreams, she decides to share her enchanting stories with the world. With every word she writes, Joanne not only unravels the rich tapestry of her imagination but also inspires others to embrace their own creative voices. Her decision to finally publish is not just about sharing tales; it is an invitation for others to embark on their own journeys of self-expression and discovery through storytelling.

While her true name will remain a tantalising secret, as she firmly believes that it adds an enchanting layer of mystery to her persona, Joanne resides in the picturesque county of Cheshire. Here, she finds inspiration in the stunning landscapes and vibrant culture that the UK has to offer. With an adventurous spirit, she loves to travel and explore the breathtaking beauty of her homeland alongside her husband, their beloved dog, and her closest friend. This close-knit circle not only accompanies her on these journeys but also plays a

Chapter One
Jarvis

In the moment of quiet introspection, Jarvis found himself pondering the recent events that had transpired. With a pensive air, he delved into his usual practice of self-reflection, carefully examining his actions and decisions. He gently probed his conscience, asking himself thoughtful questions to gauge his contentment with the outcomes, and to assess the wisdom of his choices. As he ruminated, Jarvis considered the paths not taken, weighing the potential consequences of alternative decisions. Jarvis explored the nuances of each situation, seeking to understand the motivations behind his actions and the ripple effects they might have caused. In this contemplative state, he aimed not just to evaluate his past but to glean insights that might guide his future choices. He always strived for personal growth and a deeper understanding of himself and the world around him. This is what made Jarvis good at what he does.

The incident at the club was traumatic for Blythe, who had suffered such profound losses, twenty men was a lot to lose. It's deeply saddening to think of the pain and grief he must be experiencing. Jarvis's decision to personally escort Blythe home showed great empathy and understanding. Despite the severity of Blythe's actions, Jarvis recognized the humanity in him and the importance of preserving his dignity in such a vulnerable moment. This act of kindness demonstrates Jarvis's compassionate nature and his belief in second chances. Tomorrow Blythe will attend the meeting. Running into McMatters after the club fiasco has left Blythe in quite the pickle, wetting your pants in front of a crime boss is not on anyone's bucket list! But fear not, because Jarvis felt sorry for him, our knight in slightly tarnished armour, is offering to give him a lift home. This small act of kindness might be the silver lining Blythe needs to begin emerging from his pit of embarrassment and onto the road to recovery. Let's hope this experience, though painful, will lead to growth and positive change for Blythe, and that Jarvis's compassion will help pave the way for a more understanding and forgiving community. Inwardly, Jarvis was exultant over the outcome. It was a monumental win for him and his trusty colleague, McMatters. As if that weren't enough, the Bennetts and Santos crime families were grinning like Cheshire cats at the outcome.

Keeping the peace among these rival criminal factions is like juggling flaming swords, while riding a unicycle on a tightrope between two skyscrapers....one wrong move, and its chaos! Yet, somehow, against all odds, Jarvis pulled it off. Even with Blythe's myriad troubles swirling like confetti in a tornado, Jarvis couldn't shake the feeling that he'd just aced an exam nobody thought he could pass, an impossible test that would make even the most seasoned scholars weep in despair. He chuckled to himself over this absurdly successful situation. He saw himself as a kind of rogue hero, a blend of Robin Hood and comic relief, who could outsmart both fate and peril with just a wink and a perfectly timed joke. His imagination painted him as someone who faced challenges with humour and courage, always finding a way to bring light even in the darkest moments.

Jarvis couldn't help but feel a twinge of sadness though, mostly because he had no one to share the victory with. McMatters and Lorraine seemed to be a perfect match for one another. McMatters had found someone special to share his life with, while Jarvis remained alone. As he contemplated his own romantic prospects, Jarvis couldn't help but hope that this year might be the one where he too would have the opportunity to connect with someone meaningful. The sight of his friends' fulfilling relationship highlighted Jarvis's own desire for that deep, personal bond and companionship. Though he was happy for McMatters, Jarvis couldn't help but wonder if his own chance at finding that special someone was just around the corner, waiting to blossom in the year ahead.

Jarvis pulled up at the location Blythe had specified, and promptly exited the vehicle. As he stepped out, an unpleasant stench immediately wafted towards him the pungent odour of stale urine lingered in the air, causing Jarvis to feel a strong urge to gag. Yet, he managed to suppress this visceral reaction and maintain his composure. Jarvis then headed back to his empty mansion, keeping all the windows down in a desperate attempt to rid his senses of the foul smell that had permeated the car. The journey home was filled with a sense of relief, as he sought to distance himself from the unpleasant olfactory experience and return to the comfort and familiarity of his own abode.

Chapter Two
McMatters

McMatters felt a deep sense of relief as the attack on the club finally ended. He knew the threat of future assaults was always present, but for now, this crisis had been resolved. With the immediate danger behind him, McMatters eagerly anticipated returning home to take some desperately needed time to unwind and decompress from the ordeal. Yet, despite this resolution, he remained on edge. His nerves were still electrified by the intense experience. His thoughts raced toward Lorraine, a beacon of hope shining through the tumult of his mind, as he desperately wished she might be awake. In this heightened state of stress and tension, every fibre of McMatters being cherished how Lorraine's mere presence could soothe his frayed nerves and help him regain his lost composure. It was as if she possessed an innate magic that could dissolve his worries and calm the storm within him. Her unwavering support transcended simple comfort; it was essential for his peace of mind, a lifeline in a sea of chaos. The thought of her gentle smile and reassuring words filled him with an overwhelming sense of tranquillity, reminding him that amidst life's relentless challenges, there existed a sanctuary in her embrace, a place where he could breathe deeply once more and feel whole again. The aftermath of the attack had left McMatters in a state of heightened arousal and anxiousness. He longed for the calming presence and support of Lorraine to aid him in his efforts to unwind and find a sense of equilibrium.

The clean-up crew arrived at the club, and were taken aback by the grisly scene that confronted them. Twenty lifeless bodies lay strewn about the club, with blood spattering the walls and floors. What shocked the crew even further was the presence of a pool of urine, an unexpected and undignified detail that stood in stark contrast to the ruthless nature of the crime that had occurred. Eric Henderson, the boss of the clean-up crew, was responsible for overseeing the clean-up. In McMatters' experience, someone who commanded a crime family should maintain a composed and formidable demeanour, even in the face of such a violent incident. The fact that one of the deceased had seemingly lost control of their bodily functions suggested a profound weakness which wasn't expected within the criminal underworld. McMatters began to ponder the implications of this unexpected display of weakness, as it could potentially reveal vulnerabilities or internal conflicts within the Blythe's organization that would require altering. As McMatters contemplated the possibility of someone else taking over the management of the Blythe's' organization, a few ideas began to take shape in his mind.

The question now arising in his mind was critical, demanding careful consideration and evaluation: Who would be the most suitable candidate to run the organisation effectively, guiding it through current challenges and ensuring its continued success? This decision would have far-reaching implications, requiring an individual with the necessary skills, experience, and vision to navigate the organisation's complexities and steer it towards its strategic objectives. Selecting the right leader would be crucial in determining the organisation's future trajectory and its ability to adapt and thrive in an ever-evolving landscape.

The prospect of finding the correct individual for the Blythe's' organisation prompted McMatters to carefully consider various options and potential candidates suited for the role. McMatters acknowledged the critical importance of finding the right individual to lead their operations into the future. Recognising the need for a candidate with the optimal combination of skills, experience, and strategic vision, he embarked on a thorough search to identify the ideal person to navigate the organisation through upcoming challenges and opportunities. This proactive approach underscores McMatters' commitment to ensuring the smooth and successful continuation of their mission, driven by a charismatic individual who is capable of effectively steering the organisation towards its goals. Exploring different possibilities and evaluating potential candidates would be a critical next step for McMatters as they sought to determine the best course of action for the Blythe's' organisation. Selecting the right person to take charge would be a pivotal decision, profoundly shaping the organisation's future trajectory and overall performance. Whoever assumes this critical role would need a unique combination of qualities and capabilities to navigate the complex landscape successfully.

Firstly, the chosen individual must be a strong, authoritative figure capable of commanding respect and leading decisively. They need to be willing to make tough choices and take necessary actions without limiting themselves or ruling out viable options. This unwavering determination and adaptability are essential for guiding the organisation through potential challenges and uncertainties. Secondly, the leader must demonstrate the ability to collaborate and coordinate effectively with various families, including all the different criminal factions. Navigating these delicate relationships and balancing competing interests requires exceptional diplomatic skills and a nuanced understanding of the organisation's intricate power dynamics. Finally, the individual must answer not only to McMatters' hierarchy but also to the influential figure of Jarvis, whose oversight and approval are crucial for the leader's success. Maintaining a constructive working relationship with Jarvis while exercising independent decision-making authority is a critical aspect of the role. Choosing the right person, one who can seamlessly integrate these multifaceted responsibilities and elevate the organisation, is a pivotal decision with far-reaching implications for the organisation's future.

McMatters had been burning the midnight oil, deep in thought, weighing his options and trying to figure out the best course of action. Hours slipped away as he wrestled with various scenarios, feeling the weight of his decision pressing down on him. When the clock finally struck three in the morning, a moment of clarity washed over him he knew it was time to call it a night and get some much-needed rest. He understood all too well that a good night's sleep could work wonders for both mind and spirit, often leading to breakthroughs that eluded him during the haze of fatigue. With that realization, he made a conscious decision to revisit the issue in the morning with fresh eyes and an unclouded mind. He believed in the power of his subconscious; perhaps by allowing it to churn through thoughts while he slept, new ideas might surface, ideas that hadn't crossed his mind before amidst his late-night deliberations. This brief respite would not only provide him with an opportunity to recharge, but would also serve as fertile ground for creative thinking. McMatters hoped that when dawn broke and he awoke invigorated, he might return equipped with clearer insights and maybe even stumble upon some innovative solutions that had previously seemed just out of reach, while he was grappling with exhaustion.

Chapter Three
The Pre-Meeting

Jarvis arrived at the club around ten o'clock in the morning, and he was pleased to see that the dedicated clean-up crew had worked diligently through the night. The once blood splattered venue had been meticulously transformed, and it was clear the space would be spotless well before dinnertime. Impeccable timing, given that the head of the influential Blythe family was scheduled to meet with Jarvis and McMatters at half past two that very afternoon. The attention to detail and swift restoration of the club's pristine condition reflected the staff's professionalism and commitment to ensuring the impending high-level meeting would take place in an appropriately polished and welcoming environment. The messenger was already on their way to deliver the details for the big meeting. It looked like it was going to be a busy day at the club, but at least everything was in tip-top shape for the important guests who would be arriving later tonight. Jarvis found himself lost in thought, reflecting on the late hours he had pulled the night before and the early wake-up call that had come far too soon. It dawned on him that he really needed a strong black coffee to power through the demanding day ahead. With determination, he carefully made a pot, understanding full well that this caffeine boost was essential to tackle everything that had piled up on his plate. As he brewed the coffee, the rich and aromatic smell began to waft through the air, creating an inviting atmosphere in his otherwise hectic morning routine. It made him ponder how vital it is to strike a balance between rest and productivity; after all, one could not thrive without taking care of oneself. Finally, as he took his first sip of the freshly brewed coffee, its warmth enveloped him like a comforting embrace while its bold bitterness sharpened his focus. This simple act grounded him and provided clarity amid the chaos of the tasks awaiting him. Just as he was savouring that moment of solace, McMatters strolled into the office with an expression that unmistakably conveyed a longing for a similar pick-me-up, a reminder of how they were all navigating through their grind together in pursuit of success and sanity amidst their busy lives.

"Morning, Jarvis. I see I have great timing again." Said McMatters.

"As always. Eric and his team have done a fantastic job cleaning up from last night. I wasn't sure they would get it all done in time." Said Jarvis.

"It was a little messy but we will see him right."

"I still have a damn stench in my car, I need to get one of the lads to get it detailed. It knocked me sick."

Reflecting on the memory of Blythe wetting himself evokes a deeply sorrowful and poignant moment that resonates with an intense emotional weight. Initially, laughter may have seemed like the natural response, a nervous reaction to an uncomfortable situation. However, as time passes and we look back on that incident, it stirs within us feelings of profound sadness and empathy. The act of losing control over one's bodily functions is not merely a physical mishap; it carries with it layers of embarrassment and vulnerability, especially when it occurs in front of intimidating figures such as crime bosses. This magnifies the distressing nature of the experience, transforming what might be seen as a humorous folly into a heart-wrenching reminder of human frailty. Jarvis knew it was essential to recognize that moments like these can leave lasting scars on one's sense of dignity and self-worth. In recalling Blythe's experience, we are reminded not only of our shared humanity but also the compassion that should extend to those who find themselves in such humiliating predicaments. It serves as a poignant reminder that everyone deserves kindness and understanding during their most vulnerable moments. This is why Jarvis took Blythe home personally.

"One thing I do know Jarvis, is he can't be the head of the Blythe's family after peeing himself in front of not just us, but the Bennetts and Santos, because it shows weakness and vulnerability," said McMatters.

"I agree on that front. The question is: who will we put in his place? We killed most of his men last night, so we need an outsider who will be willing to take it on."

"My thoughts exactly. I was mulling it over most of the night. Finding the right person won't be easy."

"What if we open it up? Ask everyone who is interested to come in for a meeting. If we split it up between us, I'm sure we could get a shortlist together."

"OK, let's put the message out and see who comes forward."

Jarvis diligently passed along the important message to the designated messenger, conveying the details of the promising opportunity. With fingers crossed, Jarvis hopes that this information will pique the interest of a few potential parties and lead to positive outcomes. The careful delivery of this message represents Jarvis' thoughtful approach to facilitating this opportunity and his anticipation of a favourable response.

"Oh yes, before I forget, how do you think Lorraine did running the club? Is it something she will do on a regular basis?"

"I think she's done rather well. I wasn't too sure, but we needed someone we could trust. I was listening to how she dealt with the taxi driver, and considering she was thrown in at the deep end, she was great."

"That's great. It would be good if it was more permanent."

"I will talk with her, see if she's interested."

Chapter Four
Day Dreaming

Maxine's mind was overrun with thoughts and feelings. Her heart is simply bursting with pure happiness and excitement! Can you believe it? She's finally going to go on a date with Demetrio, this charming Italian gentleman who's swept her off her feet! It's like a dream come true! He's everything she's ever hoped for, so attentive, respectful, and oh-so-adoring. The way he treats her is just magical, showering her with all the care and affection she's always deserved. It's as if the stars have aligned to bring these two wonderful souls together. What a joyous occasion! Maxine's radiant smile says it all. She's on cloud nine, and her happiness is contagious!

My goodness, since that magical moment when Maxine stepped into his enchanting restaurant for that long-awaited date, it's like the universe itself shifted! The sheer wonder of that chance encounter has left Maxine absolutely spellbound! It's as if she's been transported to another realm, floating on cloud nine, lost in the most mesmerizing daydreams imaginable. The sheer bliss... the euphoria coursing through her veins... it's simply beyond words! Who would have thought that a single evening could ignite such an incredible, awe-inspiring whirlwind of emotions? It's like witnessing a shooting star up close, breath taking, rare, and utterly unforgettable! It's absolutely mind blowing how Maxine has stumbled upon this incredible man, Demetrio! It's as if the universe conspired to create this perfect embodiment of chivalry and romance, tailor made just for her! Demetrio is like a dream come true, fulfilling every single romantic desire Maxine has ever harboured in her heart. It's utterly breath-taking to witness such a magical connection! Who would have thought that all those qualities that she's been longing for in a partner could exist in one extraordinary person? It's like watching a real-life fairy tale unfold before our very eyes!

Demetrio was the epitome of the quintessential Italian gentleman, sweeping her off her feet with his suave mannerisms, captivating charisma, and unwavering dedication to cherishing and uplifting her in the manner she had always envisioned. Maxine felt incredibly fortunate and blessed to have serendipitously crossed paths with this truly remarkable man, and she was positively elated to have found her perfect match. Demetrio's request for Maxine's phone number from Lorraine, Maxine's daughter, filled Maxine with joy and delight. The fact that Demetrio had sought to reach out and connect with Maxine directly signalled his genuine interest and affection for her. Maxine was elated by this development, as it confirmed that Demetrio harboured feelings for her and was trying to further their relationship. This thoughtful gesture from Demetrio brought a sense of happiness and anticipation to Maxine, who looked forward to the prospect of speaking with him and exploring the possibility of a deeper, more meaningful connection.

Unfortunately, Maxine's previous romantic relationships had been fraught with disappointment and mistreatment. The men she had been involved with often displayed unattractive qualities, such as being slobbish, crude, and prone to angry outbursts or excessive drinking. Worst of all, each one of these men had physically abused Maxine, leaving her battered and bruised, and had also taken advantage of her by stealing from her. Despite the pain and trauma, she had endured, Maxine's spirit remained joyful, as she was determined to move forward and find the happiness and respect she deserved. Maxine eagerly awaited the anticipated phone call, her excitement palpable as she paced back and forth around her daughter's home. She was unsure of how best to occupy her time while overcome with a sense of giddiness akin to that of a much younger individual. Though no longer a spring chicken, Maxine found herself brimming with anticipation, her youthful enthusiasm shining through despite her advancing years.

Chapter Five
Butterfly

Lorraine sat at the kitchen's breakfast bar, amusedly observing Maxine as she paced about the room, visibly on edge. The sight of her mum's fidgety, restless movements tickled Lorraine's funny bone, as it reminded her of a nervous schoolgirl harbouring a not-so-subtle crush. Lorraine couldn't help but chuckle inwardly at Maxine's endearingly jittery antics, which she found both comical and oddly endearing.

"Good job I've not got a carpet, Mum. You would have put holes in it by now."

"I'm fine, no issues here."

"You're on tenterhooks, Mum. Sit down and relax."

Lorraine observed Maxine attempting to sit down, but her restless mum's efforts were short lived, as she jumped back up and resumed her incessant pacing after mere minutes had elapsed. Lorraine couldn't help but roll her eyes at Maxine's fidgety behaviour, and decided it was time for her to take her leave. Excusing herself, Lorraine headed upstairs to gather her belongings, eager to make her way to the club and escape Maxine's seemingly endless nervous energy. Lorraine had quite taken to the responsibility of overseeing the club's operations. It provided a refreshing change of pace from her typical illicit escapades, a much-needed respite after the harrowing near miss with the police and that unpleasant run in with the ever-troublesome Jackson. Ah, the simple pleasures of an honest day's work, free from the constant threat of being caught red-handed pilfering those dazzling, overpriced gemstones.

While the adrenaline rush of her former life still lingered, Lorraine found herself rather enjoying this newfound sense of stability and normalcy. Who would have thought she'd one day prefer balancing the books to dodging security guards and evading the long arm of the law? The other reason was McMatters... Mr. Dreamy himself... the man who had single handedly awakened a whole host of feelings and sensations within Lorraine, that she didn't even know were possible. Sure, Lorraine understood McMatters was a bit of a bad boy, but in her eyes, he was her bad boy, and that was just oh so refreshing. It was like a sweet, forbidden fruit that she just couldn't resist indulging in, no matter how much her better judgment tried to steer her away. A significant transformation had taken place in Lorraine's life, but it was for the better... something she never could have foreseen or envisioned in her wildest dreams. Remarkably, she had now found herself in the unexpected position of helping to manage a club for a real-life crime boss. It was a true "pinch me" moment, a delightful plot twist that felt almost too good to be true.

Lorraine had to chuckle at the sheer absurdity and serendipity of it all. Her life had taken such an unanticipated, yet delightfully engaging, turn. The transformation of Lorraine was truly a sight to behold, akin to witnessing a butterfly emerge from its cocoon. Never in a million years would that formerly timid Lorraine have dared to set foot on a dance floor, let alone unleash her inner showstopper and strut her stuff with such unbridled enthusiasm. But lo and behold, Lorraine went and did the unthinkable. Shaking her groove thing with such fervour, she captivated poor McMatters with a performance that would make even the most seasoned and jaded showstopper blush with envy.
It was a spectacle that defied all expectations, a true testament to the power of self-discovery and the courage to step out of one's comfort zone. It was a sight that will be forever etched in the memories of all who bore

witness to Lorraine's remarkable metamorphosis from shy bystander to dance floor diva. Lorraine, ever the picture of elegance and poise, delicately applied the final touches to her immaculately crafted makeup as she beckoned for her personal chauffeur. With a flick of her wrist and a gentle flutter of her lashes, she summoned the driver, no doubt eager to whisk her away to her next high-society engagement in the lap of luxury.

Chapter Six
Poor Blythe

Blythe felt a profound sense of dread and unease as the time approached for his meeting with McMatters and Jarvis. The thought of having to discuss his embarrassing urinary incontinence issue filled him with a deep sense of shame and discomfort that made his stomach churn. He knew this personal matter would be highly uncomfortable to address, and he worried about how his colleagues would react and perceive him if they found out. The prospect of having to confront this sensitive and humiliating problem in a professional setting weighed heavily on Blythe's mind, leaving him anxious and apprehensive about the impending meeting. Blythe found himself plagued with a growing sense of unease and uncertainty about his future. He could not help but wonder if his time had finally come to an end, and whether he still possessed the same drive and fortitude that had once made him such a formidable force to be reckoned with. The once mighty Blythe, who had always been known for his unwavering determination and fighting spirit, now found himself in a humiliating situation, unable to control his own bodily functions.

This stark contrast between his former prowess and his current state filled him with a deep sense of shame and self-doubt, leaving him to ponder whether he still had what it took to face the challenges that lay ahead.
The Blythe family, or what remained of it, was deeply distressed and outraged by the tragic events that had unfolded. They were grappling with the devastating reality that their loved ones had been killed, and they held him responsible for this devastating outcome. However, Blythe, who was at the centre of the controversy, maintained that he had not intentionally let everyone get killed. It had simply been the unpredictable

and uncontrollable nature of the situation they had found themselves in. The game they had been playing had proven to be far more treacherous and unpredictable than anyone could have anticipated, leading to a series of events that had spiralled out of control and resulted in the unthinkable.

The Blythe family were left reeling, struggling to come to terms with the immense loss and the perceived lack of accountability for what had transpired. Blythe deeply regrets his arrogance and lack of diligence, which tragically resulted in the deaths of twenty of his friends and family members. His overconfidence in his own abilities as a criminal mastermind led him to neglect thorough research and planning, a grave oversight that had devastating consequences. Blythe is now consumed by guilt and anguish, painfully aware that his reckless assumptions and inflated sense of his own capabilities, directly contributed to this horrific loss of life.

Blythe is tormented by the knowledge that had he been more cautious, responsible, and attentive to detail, this catastrophic outcome could have been prevented. Blythe's failure to exercise proper care and foresight has left him wracked with remorse and a profound sense of personal culpability for the needless tragedy.

Blythe sets off for the club ....

The Meeting

McMatters and Jarvis were in the office when Lorraine abruptly arrived. Without hesitation, she greeted McMatters with a tender kiss, observed his empty glass, and promptly refilled it. Turning to Jarvis, she filled his glass as well, then prepared a purple rain cocktail for herself. The effortless way Lorraine took as she confidently strode around, left McMatters and Jarvis exchanging amused glances, bursting into laughter at her approach. There was an air about Lorraine. Both men had independently arrived at the same core idea, but there were still several critical questions that they would both need to carefully consider and address. Moreover, these questions would also require thoughtful deliberation from Lorraine, who played a central role in the situation they were thinking about. The resolution of these open inquiries would be pivotal in determining the feasibility and viability of their shared concept. Reaching a mutual understanding and alignment on the key issues at hand would be essential for them to discuss and effectively move forward to make informed decisions about the ideas and implementation.

Distracting Lorraine from the laughter that echoed around her was the sight of a man trudging towards the office, his head hanging low and his shoulders hunched in a posture of dejection and humiliation. The man's defeated demeanour and downcast appearance stood in stark contrast to the jovial atmosphere, immediately drawing Lorraine's attention away from the source of the amusement.

"Guys... we have got company," said Lorraine.

McMatters and Jarvis glanced upwards towards the door, their expressions resolute and their bodies poised, prepared to spring into action at a moment's notice. The tense stillness in the air was palpable as they fixated their unwavering gaze on the entrance, anticipating the imminent arrival of whatever or whomever lay beyond. Their posture was rigid, betraying a sense of alertness and determination, as they steeled themselves for the confrontation or challenge that was sure to come through that door. Walking behind Blythe were the heads of the Bennetts and the Santos families. Both were eager to find out what Jarvis would do with Blythe.

"Blythe, do come in. Drink?" said McMatters, who tried hard to lighten things for Blythe.

"Thank you," Blythe said quietly.

"So, Blythe, what should we do about this situation?" asked Jarvis.

"I don't know, Jarvis. All I can say is how sorry I am."

"Well, that's good to know, Blythe, but some things do concern me. First, you didn't do your research. Next, most of your men are no longer with us. Then, there's the accident." said Jarvis.

"I know." said Blythe sinking further into the chair.

"From where I'm sitting, when a crime boss is standing in front of you, the last thing on earth you should do is wet yourself." said Lorraine cutting the air with a knife.

Blythe was overcome with emotion, silent tears streaming down his face. Lorraine quickly and compassionately offered him a box of tissues, recognizing his distress. Jarvis and McMatters, seemingly unaware of the tissues' presence in the office, watched the scene unfold with uncertainty, unsure of how to respond to their Lorraine's offering to the vulnerable display of emotion by Blythe.

"Blythe, I know how hard this must be right now. With so much loss, I truly feel your pain." said Lorraine.

McMatters gaze darted between Lorraine, Jarvis, the Bennetts, the Santos and Blythe, expressing a palpable sense of shock. Lorraine's actions were nothing short of masterful, with one hand, she delicately offered tissues to Blythe, while the other wielded a metaphorical sledgehammer, striking him with unwavering force and precision. This display of contrasting behaviours was not only clever, but also undeniably impactful, leaving a lasting impression on all who witnessed it.

"Let's see if we can work something out, but you do know it's over, don't you?" said Lorraine which was like delivering another whack.

This time, Jarvis was the one left utterly gobsmacked, silently turning to face each person in the room with a shell-shocked expression. He finally locked eyes with McMatters, who was staring back at him with a similarly amazed look. For the first time, both men nodded in shared astonishment as they witnessed Lorraine systematically dismantle and destroy Blythe. Even the other families were surprised at Lorraine's approach.

"How about this Blythe. We take over your family empire and all dealings go through us. Deals are approved by us; you stay in for face value with your contacts, but you don't run the ship. Daily, and I do mean daily meetings with updates supplied by you Blythe. In return you save face on the recent loss and failings, and you get to keep a percentage of any profits," said Lorraine. It was like taking candy from a baby and dangling it in front of their face.

"I... um... I...." Blythe stuttered and mumbled not knowing what to say.

McMatters and Jarvis were eagerly anticipating Blythe's agreement, as it would mean a significant reduction to their workload and a bigger share of the profits. The prospect of having less work to handle filled the employees of McMatters and Jarvis with a sense of excitement and relief. They sat on the edge of their seats, anxiously awaiting Blythe's decision, knowing that his approval would translate to a more manageable and efficient workflow for the entire team.

Oh boy, Lorraine pulled off a real hocus-pocus number here! She's like a ninja in a business suit, sneaking around in the shadows, making money appear out of thin air. Ka-ching! But wait, there's more! The pièce de résistance was how she served Blythe a slice of humble pie with a side order of "take that!" It's like she waltzed into his office, did a little tap dance on his ego, and moonwalked out with a briefcase full of cash. Talk about a magical money dance! Lorraine for President of Sneaky Shenanigans, am I right?

The thing is McMatters and Jarvis were going to ask for this with Blythe, but they were asking for participation as a curtesy, where Lorraine just took it without asking, no warning no communication then at last minute say do you agree....? Yet Blythe knew he had no choice.

"Yes ok," said Blythe.

"That settles it then," said Lorraine.

She got up positioned herself so he had to get up, she guided him to where she wanted him and just walked him out of the door, past the Bennetts and the Santos, then shut the door behind him.

"What an idiot," said Lorraine.

Oh boy, McMatters, Jarvis, Bennett and Santos were in stitches for a solid three quarters of an hour, giggling like schoolkids every time they glanced at Lorraine. Little Miss No-Nonsense strutting around, demanding things left and right and pushing our poor clueless Blythe's buttons like she's playing Whack-a-Mole at the county fair. And the best part? Blythe had absolutely no clue she was pulling his leg! It was like watching a cat try to catch a laser pointer utterly hilarious and completely futile. Talk about a comedy goldmine!

Chapter Seven
The Office

"Lorraine, what can I say? That was masterful, the way you handled Blythe, took the mickey out of him, then had him like putty in your hands. Nice job," said Jarvis.

"Honey, you did fantastic. We weren't sure how to deal with him. How did you know what we needed?" asked McMatters.

"Oh, I heard you as I was on my way into the office. Knew what you wanted but felt for him as well. Figured you needed a female touch," said Lorraine.

"I found it entertaining to say the least," said Bennett.

"Oh, I couldn't agree more," said Santos.

"We are a great team, and I think if you're up for it, your position here in the club should be more permanent," said Jarvis. "Steve, are you okay with this?"

"Most definitely. You brought something to the table that surprised us both. How would you like to be Blythe's handler?" asked McMatters.

"Really?" said Lorraine.

"Yes, Lorraine. You've got what we need, and you know how to make Blythe dance to your tune without making him feel foolish and stupid. What do you say?"

"Okay, yes! I'm guessing I'll still be working at the club?"

"Yes."

"Woohoo! I feel the need to shop. Got to look the part!" Lorraine dashed out of the office.

McMatters and Jarvis erupted into a fit of laughter, knowing full well that their devious plan would serve them well. After all, they didn't exactly have an abundance of people they could trust, and certainly not many who could pull off the daunting task of leading a notorious mob family. Both McMatters and Jarvis exchanged a mischievous glance, relishing in the delicious irony of their situation. A couple of scoundrels about to become the big shots in charge of a criminal enterprise. It was almost too good to be true, and they couldn't help but chuckle at the sheer audacity of their scheme.

"I'm off now guys. It was an interesting meeting, speak soon," said Bennett.

"I will walk out with you Bennett, talk later," said Santos, who nods to McMatters and Jarvis.

Jarvis and McMatters needed to transform a designated space just for Lorraine, it would be a nice surprise for her. After all, she could no longer justify commandeering poor McMatters' desk as her personal vanity station. Determined to make Lorraine's new domain worthy of her exquisite tastes, the dynamic duo enlisted the help of their trusty assistant.

Paulie with a twinkle in his eye, while Lorraine went shopping, he set about sorting Lorraine an area in the office. Paulie carefully selected Lorraine's favourite tipple, a bottle of the ever chic "Purple Rain." But the pièce de resistance was the high-heel decanter and matching female body-shaped glasses Paulie had procured, ensuring Lorraine's new nook would be a sanctuary of style and sophistication befitting the office's resident diva. Her desk was a gleaming, pristine white, its high gloss finish practically blinding anyone who dared to gaze upon it. But the real showstopper was the chair, a vibrant, rich purple leather throne that seemed to have been plucked straight from the set of a Prince music video. As she would sit perched upon this royal seat, sipping on her matching "Purple Rain" cocktail, she would exude an air of effortless style and sophistication that would make even the most fashionable of office divas green with envy.

"Paulie, you have done a fantastic job! It's perfect. Lorraine is going to love it!" said McMatters.

McMatters had been eagerly anticipating Lorraine's reaction to the surprise they had meticulously arranged. While McMatters took care of the overall setup, they felt confident that Lorraine's impeccable eye for design would flawlessly handle the remaining decor and furnishings. After all, Lorraine's talent for curating visually stunning environments was practically legendary among their social circle. McMatters couldn't wait to see Lorraine's face light up with delight as they unveiled their collaborative masterpiece.

Shopping Spree

Lorraine was absolutely thrilled about her brand-new job opportunity. Up until this point, she hadn't really held down many positions that were a great fit for her unique skillset and personality. But now, Lorraine was going to be working at the local club and essentially running one of the local crime families. Talk about a dream job! She felt a sense of power and control that she had never experienced before. Lorraine could basically boss this guy around and make him do anything she wanted, and he would be reporting directly to her from now on. Oh, the satisfaction and exhilaration she felt in this moment was like nothing she had ever known. For once in her life, Lorraine was truly feeling empowered and in charge. This was going to be one wild ride, that's for sure!

Lorraine knew she needed to look the part for the occasion, so she enlisted the help of her trusted security team to ensure she was properly attired. The crew was on standby, ready to spring into action if needed. Not that Lorraine expected any trouble, of course. After all, this was the same group that had safeguarded her during her previous high-profile event, and they had proven themselves more than capable of handling any unexpected situations that might arise. Lorraine couldn't help but feel a sense of comfort and confidence, knowing her seasoned security detail had her back, no matter what the day might have in store for them.

Finding the perfect suit that checks all the boxes, a flattering fit, comfort, and impeccable style, can be a real challenge, as Lorraine knows all too well. But when Lorraine stumbled upon that light blue dream suit, with its deeper blue accents on the collar, cuffs, and pockets, it was love at first sight. The satin fabric felt divine against her slim, curvaceous figure, though Lorraine knew full well that delicate materials like satin and silk can be merciless on those of us not blessed with the physique of a runway model. Still, Lorraine couldn't resist the allure of that stylish, sophisticated ensemble, determined to rock it with all the confidence of a seasoned fashionista, regardless of any minor figure flaws the clingy fabric might accentuate. After all, when you look this good, who needs forgiveness? Lorraine found some deep blue shoes and bag to match as she was on her way to the till.

The next couple of shops had not panned out quite as well as she had hoped, so Lorraine decided it was time to take a much-needed coffee break. She made her way to the charming Italian café down the street, signalling for her security detail to join her. After all, if they were going to be shadowing her every move, she might as well get to know them a bit better. The least she could do was treat them to a round of cappuccinos or espressos. After all, they were working hard to keep her safe, and a little caffeine was the least she could provide.

"Come join me?" asked Lorraine.

"Sorry, Lorraine. While on duty, we can't leave our post, but we will accept the coffee. We must wait outside, though."

"Totally understandable," said Lorraine.

Lorraine sat at the café, sipping her morning coffee and pondering her next move in the eternal quest for the perfect suit. She gazed pensively into the depths of her steaming mug, as if the answers to her sartorial dilemma might be revealed in the swirling patterns of cream and foam. With a heavy sigh, she mentally scrolled through the endless options the stuffy department stores, the pretentious boutiques, the cavernous outlets. None of them seemed quite right. Lorraine knew her hunt for the holy grail of business attire would require another expedition, another day of trying on outfit after outfit, each one less flattering than the last. But she was determined, coffee in hand and credit card at the ready, to soldier on in her noble quest for the suit that would make her feel like a million bucks, even if it cost her that much to acquire it.

So, Lorraine, ever the determined shopper, decided to make one more stop, crossing her fingers in the hope that this final retail establishment would finally have the perfect item that she had been searching for. With a gleam in her eye and a spring in her step, Lorraine boldly ventured forth, ready to put her keen eye and bargaining skills to the test once more, fully convinced that lady luck would smile upon her this time around. Lorraine was on a mission, scouring the high street in search of the perfect attire. As she approached the last shop, a general clothing store, she couldn't help but feel a twinge of scepticism. "Really? This is my last hope?" she muttered under her breath. Mustering up her courage, Lorraine stepped inside and began browsing the racks. To her surprise, she stumbled upon a trifecta of sartorial delights a grey suit, a white suit, and a shockingly pink ensemble. "Pink? Me? Absolutely not!" she exclaimed, her inner fashionista recoiling at the thought. But then, Lorraine's fingers traced the soft, luxurious fabric of the grey suit, and she couldn't resist trying it on. "Ooh, the fit is divine!" she exclaimed, twirling in front of the mirror. Next, she slipped into the pristine white number, admiring the way the silver collar and pockets complemented her complexion.

With her newfound fashion finds in hand, Lorraine set out to complete her ensemble, searching for the perfect shoes and bag to tie the whole look together. "Watch out, world," she declared with a grin, "Lorraine is about to make a statement!" Lorraine scanned the room, her eyes landing on a shiny, silver twist-knot handbag that immediately caught her attention. "Aha, perfect!" she exclaimed, her face lighting up with delight. Continuing her hunt, she stumbled upon a pair of shoes with a delightfully twisted front design, a match made in fashion heaven! "These will go splendidly with both of my outfits," Lorraine mused, already picturing herself strutting down the street, accessorized to the nines.

Unfortunately, Lorraine's feet were protesting at this point, crying out for mercy after a long day of shopping. "Alright, alright, I hear you," she sighed, conceding defeat. "Time to call it a day and head home to put my weary tootsies up." With one final longing glance at her new-found treasures, Lorraine made her way to the exit, already dreaming of the next shopping adventure.

Well, well, well! Look who's turned over a new leaf! Our dear Lorraine, the queen of five-finger discounts, just had her first shopping trip without any sticky-fingered shenanigans. Can you believe it? Lorraine is so shocked; you'd think she'd accidentally walked out wearing clothes! Now, the million-dollar question (or should we say, the "not-stolen" question): Has our Lorraine finally found her moral compass, or is she just getting her kicks elsewhere?

Maybe she's discovered the adrenaline rush from dealing with crime bosses who wet themselves. Who knows? Perhaps she's graduated from petty theft to grand larceny and is now planning an Ocean's Eleven-style heist or a murder or two! Whatever the reason, let's raise a glass (that we actually paid for) to Lorraine's unexpected bout of honesty. Here's hoping it's not just a phase, or her next shopping trip might involve a complimentary pair of silver bracelets... courtesy of the local police department!

The Club

Lorraine arrived at the club, enthusiastically greeting staff as she walked through the entrance. With a warm smile and a friendly demeanour, Lorraine made sure to acknowledge and welcome each person she passed, creating a welcoming and lively atmosphere as she made her way into the club. Her vibrant and outgoing personality shone through, setting the tone for an enjoyable and engaging experience for all those around her.

"Looking good, Miss Spencer!" said Paulie, amidst the lively preparations for the evening's opening. The dedicated individual was hard at work meticulously setting up the bar. With a keen eye for detail and a passion for hospitality, this energetic bartender was diligently arranging the glassware, organizing the liquor bottles, and ensuring that every aspect of the bar was ready to welcome the eager club goers. The air was filled with a sense of anticipation as this skilled professional put the final touches to the bar. He eagerly awaited the arrival of the first guests and the opportunity to showcase his expertise in crafting delightful cocktails and providing an exceptional customer experience.

"Paulie, please call me Lorraine."

Lorraine eagerly made her way up the stairs, filled with excitement as she approached the office where Jarvis and McMatters were already waiting. As soon as she laid eyes on McMatters, Lorraine felt a surge of pure delight. He looked stunning tonight in his sleek, black power suit, which accentuated his impeccable style and refined fashion sense. Lorraine couldn't help but feel incredibly fortunate to be with such a handsome, well-groomed man. His cleanly shaven face was as smooth and flawless as a baby's delicate skin. Lorraine couldn't help but be utterly enthralled by McMatters' striking appearance. His light brown locks, floppy and styled with a carefree elegance, were beautifully highlighted, adding a touch of effortless sophistication that only heightened his already captivating presence. Lorraine found herself completely smitten, basking in the sheer joy and delight of being in McMatters' captivating company. His alluring looks, combined with an undeniable charm, had Lorraine feeling completely enamoured and enchanted. Her heart fluttered with excitement and anticipation at the prospect of spending more time in this magnetic individual's captivating aura. Lorraine walked into the office and was immediately stopped in her tracks, overcome with a sense of sheer delight and amazement. As she spun around, she was utterly gobsmacked to discover that McMatters and Jarvis had thoughtfully added a brand-new desk, just for her!

The desk was a stunning piece, boasting a sleek and modern white high-gloss finish that immediately caught her eye. But the true showstopper was the chair that accompanied the desk. It was like something straight out of a fairytale! Lorraine couldn't help but be captivated by the rich, vibrant hue of purple that perfectly complemented the desk's pristine appearance. Her excitement only grew as she noticed the truly unique and whimsical piece that sat atop the desk... a decanter in the shape of a high heeled shoe! This was no ordinary decanter; it had a body shaped glasses, creating a truly one-of-a-kind and utterly delightful feature. Lorraine could hardly contain her enthusiasm and joy at the thoughtful and impeccably designed workspace that had been created just for her. She was completely enamoured by the attention to detail and the clear effort put forth by McMatters and Jarvis to craft such a personalized and enchanting work environment. The decanter had been filled with a mysterious, captivating liquid that resembled nothing less than purple rain itself! Lorraine's curiosity was immediately piqued, and she simply couldn't resist the temptation to pour herself a drink and discover the true nature of this alluring, enigmatic beverage. With a sense of eager anticipation, she brought the glass to her lips, eager to indulge in this novel sensory experience and uncover the secrets hidden within the decanter's mesmerizing amethyst contents!

"You two are bad .... but oh... so good at it. I love it! Thanks!" said Lorraine.

"You're welcome. I'm glad that you approve," said Jarvis.

McMatters arrived with a spring in his step and a warm smile on his face. Without hesitation, he swept Lorraine into a passionate embrace, pulling her close. Gazing into her eyes with unbridled affection, McMatters leaned in and tenderly pressed his lips against Lorraine's, savouring the moment in a display of deep, genuine emotion. The two lovers melted into each other's arms, lost in the blissful connection of their heartfelt kiss.

Jarvis cleared his throat with a slight cough, subtly reminding the others gathered that he was still present and attentive, not wanting to be overlooked or forgotten amidst their intimate exchange. His polite yet purposeful gesture served to gently interject himself back into the discussion, ensuring his voice and perspective would not be lost or overshadowed by the lively exchange taking place around him.

As the night fell, time seemed to slip away in the blink of an eye. The vibrant club was now open and buzzing with energy, filled with the lively atmosphere that McMatters had come to cherish. Without hesitation, he headed down to the club to embark on his familiar walk around, eager to soak in the electric ambiance and connect with the enthusiastic club goers. Lorraine needed to make her first call with Blythe.

"Hello Blythe, how are things going? Remember me?" "Um... um... yes! Lorraine. Nice to hear from you." Said Blythe.

"Any issues?"

"No, rather quiet at the moment."

"Good. I'll leave you to it, but if there are any issues, and I do mean any, I want to be the first person you go to."

"OK, I will Miss Lorraine."

"Bye, Blythe. Have a good evening."

Lorraine was overjoyed that the evening had been straightforward and unencumbered by any problematic issues. As someone who was still relatively new to this endeavour, she recognized that navigating these unfamiliar waters represented a significant learning curve for her. However, the fact that she was able to get through the night without encountering any major obstacles filled her with a profound sense of relief and satisfaction. Lorraine felt a growing confidence and enthusiasm, knowing that with each passing experience, she was steadily gaining the knowledge and skills necessary to handle this role with ever increasing ease and effectiveness.

Lorraine dashed out of the office and put one of her new suits on in the bathroom. She strode back in with a confident flare and capped it off with a whirl in the middle of the office.

"Damn Lorraine that looks good on you" said McMatters.

Chapter Eight

Lorraine's place

McMatters ached with a deep, visceral longing to see Lorraine. He craved her presence, the intimate connection of being physically close to her. It was a need that went beyond mere physical desire. He yearned to simply be with her, to bask in her companionship and feel the warmth of her being. This was a craving he had not experienced in far too long, a void in his life that demanded to be filled by Lorraine's radiant spirit and comforting embrace. The intensity of his feelings was palpable, a passionate fire burning within him that could only be quelled by reuniting with the woman who held his heart. McMatters eagerly approached Lorraine's front door, his heart racing with anticipation. He had been anxiously awaiting her return from her shopping expedition, and the sight of her car parked in the driveway confirmed that she was finally back home. With a sense of excitement and purpose, McMatters firmly pressed the doorbell, eager to greet Lorraine and learn all about her latest adventures and purchases.

Lorraine, brimming with enthusiasm, led him into the kitchen where she promptly set about preparing refreshing drinks for the pair of them. With the sun still shining brightly outside, the couple decided to venture out and settle comfortably into the plush loungers in the garden. As they sipped their beverages, Lorraine excitedly recounted the details of her recent shopping excursion, eager to share the highlights of her productive and enjoyable trip. Steve and Lorraine thoroughly savoured each other's company, delighting in the casual conversation and the breath-taking sunset that painted the sky. As they sipped the freshly prepared lemon drink, Steve was captivated by the exquisite flavour, which was flawlessly balanced and refreshing. The shared experience of this tranquil moment, enhanced by the perfect beverages, filled them both with a sense of joy and contentment. Steve was thoroughly impressed by the exceptional taste, which complemented the pleasant ambiance and the warmth of this intimate exchange.

As the sun dipped below the horizon, Lorraine could feel the temperature starting to drop, sending a slight chill through her body. Determined to escape the growing coolness, she turned to Steve and, with a sense of urgency, grasped his hand firmly. Guiding him with purpose, Lorraine led the way, swiftly ascending the stairs and leaving the chilly air behind. Steve was utterly captivated by the breath-taking design of the staircase before him. The intricate metalwork of the balustrade was nothing short of mesmerizing, with waves of graceful bends and curves that seemed to flow effortlessly, creating a sense of elegant fluidity. The thoughtful details, such as the smooth, rolled top edge that gently cradled the hand, demonstrated a level of craftsmanship that left Steve in awe.

The harmonious juxtaposition of the warm, wooden treads in shades of white and grey against the striking black of the balustrade created a stunning visual contrast, elevating the staircase to a true work of art. Steve found himself transfixed, marvelling at the sheer brilliance of the design and the skilled execution that brought this architectural marvel to life. Lorraine's actions conveyed a palpable eagerness, driven by her desire to seek refuge in the cosy confines of the home, leaving Maxine and her programs in the front room as they ascended to a more private space. Steve had never had the privilege of venturing upstairs in Lorraine's abode, and the anticipation of this rare opportunity filled him with a sense of unbridled excitement. The prospect of exploring the intimate, private spaces of her home promised to be a true delight, a chance to gain a deeper, more immersive understanding of Lorraine and her world. Steve's heart raced with a mixture of eager curiosity and the thrill of the unknown. He knew that this experience would offer a unique and intimate glimpse into Lorraine's life that few others had been granted. The sheer anticipation of this treat in store for him was palpable, fuelling his imagination and heightening his senses as he prepared to embark on this tantalizing journey.

Lorraine

Lorraine had been contemplating this moment for some time, knowing deep down that it was long overdue. She was acutely aware that Steve, had never set foot upstairs in her home, a curious oversight given the intimacy they shared. But tonight, as they had witnessed the breath-taking display of the setting sun together, Lorraine felt a growing sense of anticipation and readiness stirring within her. The vibrant hues of the sky's farewell had ignited a smouldering passion, and Lorraine knew she could no longer delay the inevitable. She was more than just ready, she was utterly consumed by a fervent, almost feverish eagerness and excitement. Her entire being brimmed with a palpable, electrifying desire to invite Steve into the private, sacred sanctum of her personal space. The prospect of finally sharing this most intimate, cherished realm of her world with the man she had grown to deeply care for filled her heart with a dizzying, overwhelming sense of anticipation. Yet, even as these powerful emotions surged within her, a flicker of uncertainty lingered. Was Steve truly the one? Was the connection they shared profound enough to constitute love, or was it still too soon to make such a profound declaration? Regardless, the pull she felt towards him was undeniable, a magnetic force that compelled her to throw caution to the wind and surrender herself completely to this blossoming romance.

At the top of the stairs, Lorraine's heart raced with excitement and anticipation. With a mischievous grin, she reached up and gently removed McMatters' tie, slowly slipping it from around his neck. Relishing the moment, Lorraine then produced a blindfold, carefully covering McMatters' eyes and depriving him of his sight. This was her chance, her opportunity to take control and indulge in a thrilling role reversal. Filled with a passionate desire to seize the moment, Lorraine was determined to have her own fun, to explore new sensations, and to savour the delicious power shift that had just taken place.

Lorraine led him intently to the sanctuary of her private quarters, positioning him near the edge of the bed. With a growing sense of passion, she leaned in and tenderly pressed her lips against his, savouring the warmth of his responsive embrace. Feeling emboldened by his reciprocation, Lorraine allowed her hands to glide delicately down the contours of his chest, deftly unfastening the buttons of his jacket one by one. The anticipation was palpable as she methodically exposed the layers beneath, her touch igniting sparks of desire within him.

Lorraine sensually slid off his jacket, deliberately and tantalizingly allowing the garment to gradually slip down his muscular arms. She savoured the moment, taking her time to peel the jacket away from his body, her fingers caressing his skin as the fabric relinquished its hold. The slow, deliberate removal heightened the tension in the air, as Lorraine's passionate gaze locked with his sightless eyes, silently communicating the intensity of her desire. Lorraine's passion ignited as she tenderly kissed and caressed her lover's neck. With a sense of eager anticipation, she slowly began undoing the buttons of his shirt, peppering his exposed skin with delicate, sensual kisses as she methodically worked her way down his torso. The intimate, electrifying touch of her lips heightened the intensity of the moment, filling the air with a palpable desire that crackled between them. Lorraine sensually traced the outline of his trousers with her delicate fingers, slowly gliding down the length of his legs all the way to his shoes.

With a tantalizing touch, she gently slipped off his footwear, revealing his bare feet and heightening the intimate, passionate moment between them. The deliberate, seductive movements of her hands ignited a smouldering desire as she meticulously undressed him, creating an atmosphere of sultry anticipation. Still blindfolded, Steve's anticipation grew palpable as Lorraine's gentle exploration of his body continued. With each caress and touch, his breath quickened, his pulse racing with mounting excitement and desire. The uncertainty of not being able to see only heightened his sensory awareness, every nerve ending igniting with an electric sensation as Lorraine's skilled hands navigated the contours of his form. The journey across his skin felt exhilarating and boundless, building a crescendo of yearning within him that threatened to spill over at any moment. Lorraine's heart raced with palpable desire as she sensually traced her fingers up his muscular thigh, the anticipation building with each tantalizing movement.

Unable to contain her passionate longing any longer, she deftly unfastened his trousers, revealing the prominent bulge that betrayed his own mounting excitement. Lorraine's eyes gleamed with wanton anticipation, eager to savour the pleasures that lay in wait. Lorraine delicately and sensually slid Steve's trousers down, meticulously ensuring they did not fall too quickly to the floor. With a passionate intensity, Lorraine then grasped the waistband of his underwear between her teeth, tugging the fabric steadily downwards and revealing his eager, throbbing arousal. The slow, deliberate unveiling of his most intimate areas created a palpable tension and desire in the air as Lorraine masterfully disrobed him. Lorraine's passionate embrace sent a jolt of excitement through Steve's body. As she tenderly kissed him, the delicate touch of her tongue caressing the sensitive tip of his arousal drove him wild with desire. The tantalizing sensations she elicited through her skilled, teasing ministrations left him gasping in pleasure, his every nerve ending alight with the intensity of her affections. Lorraine's amorous attentions ignited a feverish response, her lover's body quivering with unbridled arousal under her masterful touch. Lorraine had stripped him of his clothes, leaving him completely unclothed and vulnerable. With a passionate intensity, she guided him to sit down on the edge of the bed, her movements deliberate and purposeful. Lorraine then climbed onto him, straddling his lap, her legs on either side of his body, as she sought to close the distance between them. The tension in the air was palpable, charged with a raw, primal energy that crackled with anticipation. She seductively positioned herself, tantalizing him with the mere proximity of her intimate curves. Teasingly, she grazed the tip of his throbbing arousal, allowing just the slightest sensation of her warm, welcoming entrance to be felt, driving him wild with desire and anticipation. The tantalizing, feather light touch left him aching to fully experience her passionate embrace. And then, filled with passion and desire, she reached for the bottle of lubricant, squeezing a generous amount onto her fingertips.

With a sensual touch, she began caressing and gliding her slick fingers all over the length of his throbbing arousal, ensuring every inch was thoroughly coated and glistening. All the while, she continued to tease and tantalize the sensitive tip, heightening his anticipation and pleasure. She plunged down relentlessly, her movements intense and unforgiving. The sheer force and urgency of her actions elicited a sharp, guttural gasp from him as she picked up speed, her pace becoming more and more frantic with each passing moment. The raw passion and unbridled desire fuelling her actions were palpable, driving her to push harder and faster, completely consumed by the heat of the moment. Steve moved with Lorraine; their bodies intertwined in a passionate embrace. They clung to each other tightly, their movements frantic and intense as they surrendered to the fire of their desire. Driven by an all-consuming passion, they became a singular, harmonious unit, their every motion fuelled by the heat of the moment. The air crackled with the raw, unbridled energy of their connection as they lost themselves in the throes of their passionate encounter.

The passionate, intense sensations overwhelmed their senses as they reached the pinnacle of ecstasy together. Their bodies trembled with the force of the shared climax, every nerve ending ignited by the sheer euphoria of the moment. Cries of pleasure escaped their lips, mingling together in a symphony of unbridled passion. The world seemed to fade away, leaving only the two of them caught in the throes of rapturous release, their bodies remained intimately intertwined, chests heaving as they struggled to catch their breath. Overcome by the intensity of their encounter, they were frozen in place, incapable of speech or movement. The sheer force of their connection had left them breathless, every fibre of their being consumed by the electric sensations coursing through them. In that moment, nothing else mattered but the palpable bond that bound them together, leaving them utterly transfixed and unable to do anything but surrender to the overwhelming euphoria.

Something truly magical was unfolding between McMatters and Lorraine, a delicate dance of connection and possibility that neither of them had yet fully grasped. It was as if the universe itself had conspired to bring them together in this moment, weaving an invisible thread of understanding and chemistry that sparked beneath the surface. The air around them seemed to shimmer with potential, filled with unspoken words and shared glances that hinted at a deeper bond waiting to be discovered. In their interactions, there was a warmth that transcended mere acquaintance; it was a budding friendship, or perhaps something more profound, quietly blossoming like spring flowers breaking through the frost. Each laugh shared and each story exchanged added another layer to this enchanting tapestry they were unknowingly creating together.

Maxine

Maxine settled in for her nightly routine of binge watching her favourite programs, a ritual she had grown accustomed to over the years. However, this evening, Maxine's peaceful viewing experience was disrupted by her daughter and McMatters. McMatters had come to visit Lorraine, Maxine's daughter.
The animated conversation and laughter between the two love birds was so loud that Maxine found it necessary to turn up the volume on the television to hear her show over the din. The boisterous exchange between Lorraine and McMatters was likely audible not only to Maxine, but also to the other neighbours and passers-by in the vicinity when the passionate screaming started. Maxine, who cherished the tranquillity of her evenings, found herself torn between her desire to enjoy her programs and the need to accommodate the intrusive presence of her daughter's visitor. This delicate balance between personal preferences and social obligations is a common challenge faced by many individuals in shared living situations. After the noisy commotion had finally subsided, Maxine was able to once again savour the peace and quiet, eagerly anticipating the day when she could have her own peaceful sanctuary and escape the disruptive bedroom antics that had interrupted her

44

tranquillity. Maxine yearned for a serene environment where she could fully immerse herself in her chosen program or activity without the intrusive sounds and distractions from the adjacent rooms.

The respite, however brief, allowed her to momentarily re-centre herself and look forward to reclaiming her personal space and freedom to enjoy her preferred pastimes without unwanted interference. Maxine found herself consumed by a deep, yearning desire to become intimate with Demetrio. She couldn't stop her mind from wandering, imagining the possibilities of such a connection. The mere thought of being close to him, of exploring that level of physical and emotional intimacy, was enough to send a thrill of anticipation coursing through her.

Maxine carefully considered what she might wear, how she might present herself, and the ways she could thoughtfully and sensually engage with Demetrio. This internal fantasy, though unspoken, was powerfully stirring her emotions and heightening her senses in profound and exciting ways. Perhaps Maxine could decide to spend some quality time with Demetrio one morning, prior to the start of his evening dinner service. This would provide them with an opportunity to enjoy each other's company and partake in an enjoyable activity or outing, allowing Demetrio a brief respite from the demands of his busy work schedule. Engaging in such a thoughtful gesture could lift Demetrio's spirits and foster a stronger, more meaningful connection between the two of them.

Chapter Nine
It's a Date

Maxine was ecstatic when Demetrio unexpectedly phoned and extended an invitation for the two of them to go out on a date together. She couldn't contain her sheer excitement, practically leaping for joy at the prospect of spending quality one-on-one time with the object of her affections. Maxine's heart was practically pounding out of her chest as she enthusiastically accepted Demetrio's proposal. She was already envisioning the romantic evening they would soon share and eagerly anticipating the opportunity to sweep him off his feet. But now, Maxine found herself in dire need of a complete image overhaul. The poor appearance of Maxine had become a true fashion disaster, leaving her feeling more like a frumpy relic from a bygone era than the stylish, put together professional she aspired to be. It was time to bid farewell to the outdated wardrobe, the unflattering hairstyle, and the overall aesthetic that made her feel like she was perpetually stuck in the wrong decade. Maxine knew she needed a transformative makeover, one that would have her feeling good too.

Lorraine had just settled down with her morning brew, savouring the first sip of the warm, aromatic liquid, when suddenly, Maxine came bursting into the room, bouncing around with the boundless energy of an exuberant schoolgirl.

"Lorraine, you'll never guess what!" Maxine exclaimed, her eyes sparkling with excitement. "I've got a date!" she announced, twirling and pirouetting as if she were the prima ballerina of a prestigious dance troupe.

"Let me finish my brew, then we'll hit the salon and get you spruced up for your date. It's about time you had a makeover!"

Maxine

Maxine had spoken with Demetrio a few times since their previous encounter at the dinner with her daughter Lorraine, though she remained uncertain about his true intentions. Was he genuinely interested in her, or simply a lonely soul seeking companionship? Maxine couldn't help but wonder, as she found herself surprisingly open to the idea of simply basking in Demetrio's company, regardless of the nature of his feelings. After all, in these trying times, a little friendly interaction could go a long way in soothing one's soul, and Maxine was more than willing to be that soothing balm, should Demetrio so desire. Maxine found herself in a quandary, unsure whether to seize the initiative and ring up Demetrio for a dinner date, or to sit back and let him do all the heavy lifting.

Her daughter Lorraine had some strong opinions on the matter, firmly asserting that the only relationships destined for success are those where the man actively pursues the woman. Perhaps this age-old wisdom could shed some light on Maxine's romantic woes. Could it be that her tendency to chase the men had been her downfall all along? With Lorraine's sage advice ringing in her ears, Maxine contemplated her next move, wondering if a more assertive approach might finally be the key to finding lasting love.

Lorraine, ever the daughter, had graciously offered to take the fashionably challenged Maxine on a much-needed shopping expedition. Maxine's wardrobe had been stuck in a time warp, with pieces dating back nearly a decade. The once stylish garments had undergone so many hastily executed repairs that they had devolved into little more than a collection of glorified rags. Lorraine knew it was high time to revamp Maxine's look and drag her kicking and screaming into the present day, whether Maxine liked it or not.

Maxine couldn't help but ponder the idea of Lorraine offering her a much-needed makeover as well. After all, Maxine felt like she was in desperate need of a fresh start, and a little pampering from her daughter might just be the trick to revitalizing her look and her spirits. She imagined Lorraine whisking her off to the salon, insisting on a complete style overhaul from a chic new haircut to a wardrobe refresh that would have Maxine feeling like a brand-new woman. The very thought had Maxine giddy with anticipation, already picturing herself strutting down the street with a newfound confidence, leaving her old self firmly in the rear-view mirror. Maxine waited for Lorraine....

Within an hour, Maxine and Lorraine found themselves at the local salon, a place that Maxine had never visited. Giddy with excitement, Maxine could hardly contain her enthusiasm as she eagerly anticipated the pampering and indulgence that awaited her. Having spent her days toiling away at mundane tasks, she was more than ready to treat herself to a much-needed spa day, where she could finally kick back, relax, and emerge looking and feeling her absolute best.

"Full makeover for Mum, please? I will just have my nails."

Maxine found herself rather unexpectedly swept up in the whirlwind of the salon, as the stylists descended upon her unruly mane, determined to tame its wild ways. Meanwhile, Lorraine sat calmly, indulging in a bit of pampering of her own. She reclined with her hands outstretched, allowing the nail technician to work their magic, transforming her digits into a veritable work of art. By the time Maxine's transformation was complete, she was practically unrecognizable. Gone was the unkempt, wild mane of hair, the pale, blemished complexion, and the non-existent nails that had once been her trademark. In their place emerged a polished, put together version of Maxine, one that could have easily graced the cover of a high-end fashion magazine. Her hair, once a tangled mess, was now neatly trimmed into a chic, manageable style, the previously grey strands now a warm, rich brown hue that complemented her features. And those nails! They had been lovingly manicured, elongated, and adorned with a classic French tip that screamed "high maintenance" in the most fabulous way possible. Maxine had truly undergone a head-to-toe makeover, emerging as a polished, well-kept vision of her former self one that even she would have a hard time recognizing.

"Demetrio won't recognise me." Maxine protested.

"Let's go get you dressed for the occasion, mum."

Operation Maxine

Lorraine knew her dear old mum Maxine had been feeling a bit under the weather lately, so she decided to concoct a sure-fire plan to lift her spirits. First, she whisked Maxine off on a wild shopping extravaganza, letting her mum indulge in a little retail therapy. Maxine had been through the wringer recently, and Lorraine knew it would take some serious coaxing to get her out and about enjoying life again. But Lorraine was determined to put a big smile back on her mum's face, makeover montage straight out of a cheesy rom com. With a fresh hairdo and a fresh set of nails, Lorraine was certain Maxine would be feeling fabulous and ready to take on the world once more. All in a day's work for this mischievous daughter!

"I'm ready for a shopping trip can you pick us up please?"

"On my way Lorraine."

"OK mum the driver is on his way."

"Driver? Are we going in style?"

"Yes mum."

"Oooh, I feel like a queen."

The driver arrived, and Maxine couldn't contain her excitement at the prospect of being chauffeured around. She positively bounced with glee, practically leaping up and down like an overjoyed child on Christmas morning. The idea of having a personal driver at her beck and call filled Maxine with a sense of pure, unadulterated delight. It was as if all her transportation dreams had come true in that singular moment.

"Ring me when your finished Lorraine, I will come to collect you both."

And with that, the driver swiftly departed.
Lorraine and Maxine started shopping, but poor Maxine was in a sartorial conundrum. After the third round of "umm" and "ahhh," Lorraine couldn't help but wonder what on earth was transpiring. Was Maxine's wardrobe malfunctioning? Had a fashion emergency erupted? Lorraine's curiosity was piqued as she observed Maxine's increasingly frantic outfit deliberations, no doubt grappling with the age-old dilemma of "what to wear?" in the most dramatic of fashions.

"Mum, why are you struggling to pick clothes to buy?"

"Well, I... um... they cost so much since I last bought any clothes."

"You're silly. This is on me, Mum. I'm buying."

"No, no, you can't."

"Yes, I am, and that's final."
Lorraine meticulously curated a wardrobe's worth of stylish garments, carefully handpicking each item for her fashionable Mum, Maxine. Maxine's closet was about to get a major upgrade, thanks to Lorraine's keen eye for the latest trends and her uncanny ability to match Maxine's personal flair. With an armful of colourful blouses, flattering dresses, and the perfect pair of statement heels, Lorraine was determined to transform Maxine into a veritable style icon, whether Maxine liked it or not.

"OK, into the dressing room you go. Let's see how they look on you."

Maxine, ever the diligent shopper, knew better than to try and argue with Lorraine. With a resigned sigh, she dutifully marched into the cramped, fluorescent lit enclosure to begin the age-old ritual of "the great clothing hunt."

First, the too big options. Billowing monstrosities that threatened to swallow her whole. Then, the one style that seemed to have been shrink wrapped directly onto her body, restricting her movements like a boa constrictor. But ah, the sweet relief when she finally unearthed that elusive fourth garment, a veritable Goldilocks approved masterpiece! Maxine couldn't help but strut out of that dressing room, positively beaming as she showcased her newfound fashion triumph. A flowing, floral adorned dress with just the right amount of shoulder coverage and a delightfully loose, airy fit. It was as if the shopping gods had smiled down upon her that day, gifting her the sartorial equivalent of a warm hug.

"Oh, that looks great, Mum! That's a definite yes."

"You think? Don't I look fat in this?"

"Nope, it's perfect."

"Oh, okay."

Maxine hurried back into the dressing room, eager to try on the next ensemble. This one was a stylish, navy-blue pantsuit with a built-in vest top seamlessly integrated into the jacket. As she slipped into the loose fitting yet tailored attire, Maxine couldn't help but marvel at the wonderfully soft and lightweight material. Feeling like a fashion mogul, she strutted out of the fitting room, ready to strut her stuff and wow the unsuspecting onlookers.

"Mum, that looks really good on you. I wonder if we could find it in more colours."

"A baby blue or other pastel colours might be nice. Put that in the 'yes' pile. I'll find more colours while you put the next outfit on."

Lorraine, ever the adventurous fashionista, embarked on a vibrant quest to expand her colour palette. Meanwhile, Maxine decided to make a bold statement, slipping into a dress that was the vivacious hue of a freshly squeezed lemon. The form fitting garment clung to her curves, stopping just above her knees, and she paired it with a crisp, ivory jacket to complete the eye-catching ensemble. Maxine surveyed her reflection in the mirror, feeling a tinge of self-consciousness creep up as she took in the ensemble adorning her figure. The outfit, while not entirely in keeping with her usual style, possessed a certain flair that piqued her interest and sparked a mischievous glint in her eye. "Well, aren't I just the talk of the town," she mused, suppressing a playful smirk as she gave a playful little spin, the fabric swishing around her legs. Sure, it was a departure from her comfort zone, but Maxine couldn't deny the thrill of trying something new, even if it left her wrestling with a touch of sartorial insecurity. After all, fashion was about having fun and expressing one's unique personality, and this look was growing on her by the minute.

"Oh, mum you look lovely."

"It's not too short?"

"No, it's a good length, I found you a peach, baby blue and a cream in the other outfit."

"You're spending too much on me."

"Don't be silly."

Maxine grimaced at the towering piles of clothing before her. Each item seeming to silently taunt her dwindling bank balance.

"Oh, this is going to cost Lorraine an arm and a leg," she muttered.

Envisioning the savings account being drained faster than a thirsty camel in the Sahara. With a sigh, she mentally prepared herself for the financial haemorrhage that was about to occur, already dreading the moment Lorraine would have to hand over her hard-earned cash to the merciless retail gods. The last outfit Maxine tried on was a perfect fit, with the jeans hugging her curves in all the right places and the top flattering her figure like a second skin. However, Maxine didn't wear it out just to show off to her daughter Lorraine. No, Maxine simply added the ensemble to her growing "keep" pile, content in the knowledge that she had found another winning look without having to try too hard. Lorraine had gathered more stuff this time it was a pile of shoes and sandals as well as a few handbags and purses, two pairs of sunglasses to match a hat and the final items were pieces of jewellery. Not real ones, just a few pieces to match the outfits.

"Okay, pick some new underwear and bras. I can't do that for you."

Maxine was absolutely exhausted after a marathon session of retail therapy. Lorraine, observing Maxine's weary expression and dragging footsteps, kindly recommended that they head back home, as it was clear Maxine had reached her shopping limit and could barely keep her eyes open, let alone continue browsing the stores.

Demetrio's

Maxine arrived at Demetrio's a full fifteen minutes before their scheduled meet up time, her palms sweating profusely and her heart racing like a jackrabbit on espresso. This was uncharted territory for her, she was no stranger to the occasional casual fling, but the prospect of an actual date, complete with the potential for romance and wooing, had her more worked up than a cat on a hot tin roof. Maxine couldn't remember the last time she had been on a proper date, if ever. Her dating history consisted primarily of quick hook-ups with men, she had little to no emotional investment in. But here she was, primped and primed, anxiously awaiting Demetrio's arrival, wondering if she was in over her head and hoping she didn't completely botch this rare opportunity for a real, genuine connection. Demetrio, the charming owner of the local restaurant, strode to the entrance and welcomed Maxine with his signature greeting a pair of affectionate cheek kisses.

Linking her arm with his, he escorted her to a cosy, tucked away booth, where the table had been adorned in a rather peculiar, yet undeniably romantic fashion. Candles flickered softly, casting a warm glow, but the vase sitting at the centre remained stubbornly flowerless, leaving one to wonder if Demetrio had forgotten this crucial romantic detail or was simply trying to keep the focus on the two of them.
From behind his back, Demetrio surreptitiously produced a freshly plucked, soft pink rose, which he then proceeded to present to Maxine in a grand, sweeping gesture. As she accepted the delicate bloom, Maxine suddenly realized the reason the vase on the table had been conspicuously empty Demetrio had been patiently waiting for the perfect moment to unveil this charming, romantic surprise. Maxine, with a flourish of her delicate fingers, gently and tenderly nestled it into the waiting embrace of the ornate vase, as if the flower were a precious gem being placed in its rightful display case. She stepped back, tilting her head slightly to the side, and admired her handiwork, a self-satisfied grin spreading across her face.

"Oh, Demetrio thank you, they are lovely."

"You look wonderfully beautiful."

"You are a romantic wonderful man, Demetrio."

Maxine and Demetrio savoured every bite of their delectable Italian feast, tucked away in the intimate, cosy booth. The two lovebirds relished not only the mouth-watering pasta and wine, but also each other's delightful company, giggling and sharing inside jokes like a couple of teenagers on a first date. The warmth of the dimly lit restaurant and the rich aromas of garlic and herbs only heightened the romantic ambiance, as Maxine and Demetrio basked in the joy of their special evening together.

Chapter Ten
McMatters' place

McMatters was in the middle of getting ready to go work at the club when there was a knock at his bedroom door. When he answered, Jeffrey stood there.

"Sorry to disturb you, boss, but a woman downstairs says she knows you and urgently needs to speak to you."

"What's her name, Jeffrey?"

"Miss Karen Sturgess."

McMatters' face suddenly drained of colour, a stark and unmistakable indicator of his mounting unease and deep-seated apprehension. The moment she entered the room, he was taken aback; he couldn't have anticipated her audacity in daring to confront him directly. It was as if the very air around them shifted, charged with an unspoken tension that hung heavily between them. His expression quickly darkened, betraying a mix of displeasure and irritation at her unexpected arrival, feelings that were now written all over his features like an open book. The furrow in his brow deepened as he grappled with a tumultuous swirl of emotions. Confusion mingled with annoyance, as he processed not only her presence, but also what it might signify. It became increasingly clear from his demeanour that he was far from pleased with the current situation or the unwelcome intrusion into what should have been a moment of solitude for him. The atmosphere felt thick with discomfort, and one could almost sense the weight of unspoken words hanging in the air. They were begging to be addressed yet somehow remaining locked away in both their hearts.

"Thank you, Jeffrey,"

McMatters descended the stairs with a heavy heart, seeking Karen in the hallway. As he approached her, he couldn't help but notice that her appearance had taken a noticeable turn for the worse, compared to how vibrant and composed she used to be. The once radiant woman who effortlessly carried herself with grace, now appeared somewhat dishevelled, revealing signs that she had let herself go. It was painfully clear that she was no longer maintaining the same level of care and attention to her personal presentation that had once defined her. This apparent decline in her grooming habits, likely hinted at deeper issues or challenges lurking beneath the surface, struggles that were weighing heavily on her spirit. Perhaps these difficulties had become so overwhelming, that they had sapped her energy and motivation, leading to a neglect of those cherished self-care rituals, that she had once embraced wholeheartedly. The stark contrast between her current unkempt state and the polished, well-kept appearance she had previously maintained, painted a poignant picture of transformation. One not borne of choice, but rather as a reflection of troubling shifts in her circumstances or mind-set. McMatters stood there observing this profound change in Karen.
"Karen, why are you here? I thought I told you never to come here."

"Oh Steve, I thought you would want to see me given the news."

"What news, Karen?" McMatters was frustrated.

"The baby, silly. Your baby."

"I don't have any children, and I haven't been with you for five years."

"You have a child, Steve."

"Before you say anything else, I want a DNA test. I don't trust you; you cheated, lied, and stole from me."

"Oh, that's in the past. We have a child together, and now we can be together again."

McMatters had been engulfed in a whirlwind of rage and indignation, following the shocking incident that had unfolded previously. The realization that the woman he once loved, known infamously as "Karen," had not only betrayed him by stealing five thousand pounds. But had also shattered his heart, by being caught in his own bed with another man, was a double blow that had left him reeling. This brazen act of theft, intertwined with profound emotional betrayal, rendered McMatters feeling deeply violated; it felt as though every ounce of trust he had placed in Karen had been mercilessly stripped away, leaving him vulnerable and exposed. As he grappled with the weight of this unsettling betrayal, McMatters found himself confronted not only by feelings of anger and hurt, but also with the daunting reality of his newfound responsibilities. The situation spiralled into an emotionally charged ordeal, that left him questioning everything he believed about love and loyalty. To complicate matters further, Karen's claim that she was raising a child who she asserts is his, added layers of confusion and distress to an already tumultuous period in his life. Faced with this challenging reality, McMatters now must navigate through a labyrinth of emotional turmoil while considering what it means to be a father under such painful circumstances. Juggling both fear and hope for the future amidst the chaos created by someone who was once so close to him.

"You will be sent an appointment for a DNA test. I want proof that the child is mine. You can leave now."

McMatters' mind was a turbulent sea of apprehension, churning with anxiety at the thought of having brought a child into the world with this woman, who seemed to embody everything he feared about such a commitment. The mere idea felt like a nightmarish scenario unfolding before him, where uncertainties loomed large, and shadows of doubt crept into every corner of his heart. He felt an overwhelming urge to gather more information, to piece together the puzzle of their situation to understand what lay ahead. It was as if he were standing on the precipice of a great unknown, desperately seeking clarity amidst swirling confusion. With a heavy heart and a growing sense of unease that weighed upon him like an anchor, McMatters opened the front door and gestured for Karen to exit his home. His body felt tense as he tried to mask his turmoil beneath a veneer of calmness; he simply wanted to put an end to this unsettling encounter. One that had left him feeling, and so off-balance. The cool air outside beckoned like a breath of fresh hope, promising respite from the emotional storm brewing within him. As she stepped over the threshold, McMatters was filled with mixed emotions. Relief intertwined with lingering uncertainty about what their futures might hold.

"Hi Jarvis, I need intel. You'll never guess who just turned up."

"You know too many to guess from. But what's up?"

"Karen. She's claiming I have had a child with her. The cheek of it! I haven't seen her for around five years. I've told her I want a DNA test. Can you get some intel on her and set up a DNA test for me, please?"

"Wow, that's huge. Of course I will."

"Thanks, Jarvis."

"Steve, does Lorraine know?"

"Oh shit! No, she doesn't."

"I'd tell her ASAP."

"I wonder what she'll say."

"Who knows, but good luck, Steve."
Jarvis puts down the phone, and McMatters knows he needs to speak with Lorraine. He had promised her that he would be honest, with no lying or cheating, as she has placed her full trust in him and everything he does. McMatters is aware that he has no choice but to be upfront with Lorraine today. He feels the weight of his previous commitments and the need to have a difficult, but necessary, conversation with her. The situation has become increasingly tense, and McMatters recognizes the importance of addressing the issues head-on, even though it may be a challenging and uncomfortable dialogue.

Honesty

Feeling a sense of urgency, McMatters hastily got into his car and sped over to Lorraine's residence. He was uncertain about what exactly he would say or how he would articulate it, but he knew that he needed to address the situation promptly. With a growing sense of apprehension, McMatters drove with a heightened sense of purpose, determined to confront the matter head-on despite his lack of a clear plan, but McMatters knew Lorraine's Rules no cheating and no lying. He didn't plan to break any of them. The situation demanded immediate attention, and McMatters was compelled to act swiftly, even if it meant navigating the encounter without a fully formulated approach. When McMatters arrived at Lorraine's residence, he firmly knocked on the door, seeking entry. Maxine, upon hearing the distinct rapping sounds emanating from the front entrance, promptly responded by approaching and opening the door, thereby granting McMatters access to their private abode and signalling her willingness to engage with him.

"Where is the fire?" asked Maxine.

"Is Lorraine still here?"

"Yes, come in, don't just stand there."

McMatters' anxiety was palpable as he cautiously entered Lorraine's place, and it felt as though the air itself was thick with his trepidation. The tension in his body was nearly tangible; an almost visible trembling overtook his frame, betraying the inner turmoil that churned within him. Every step he took seemed weighted by the gravity of the situation he was about to face, sending ripples of unease through him. His mind raced with a thousand thoughts, each one more daunting than the last, leaving his nerves frayed and his composure teetering on the brink of collapse. As McMatters crossed the threshold into Lorraine's house, his demeanour spoke volumes. A profound sense of unease and apprehension radiated from him, like heat waves on a scorching day. He instinctively scanned the room for signs of comfort or familiarity but found none; instead, uncertainty loomed large around him. The prospect of whatever awaited him inside stirred an unsettling cocktail of fear and anticipation in his gut, making it all too clear that he was grappling with an emotional storm. Struggling to maintain his composure amidst overwhelming anxiety, McMatters took a deep breath in a futile attempt to steady himself against the tide of worry that threatened to engulf him entirely.

"Steve, are you OK?" asked Lorraine.

"We need to talk."

"Follow me," Lorraine replied.

Lorraine gently guided McMatters to the outdoor table, nestled in the tranquil garden. With a warm smile and a steadying hand, Lorraine carefully escorted him as they made their way to the peaceful, sun dappled setting beyond the back door. The garden, with its vibrant flowers and soothing ambiance, provided the perfect quite location where no one could over hear what was said.

"Mum, can you get us some drinks please?"

Maxine excused herself to go and prepare beverages for Lorraine and McMatters, ensuring their discussion could proceed in a confidential manner. Lorraine then took the initiative to firmly close the patio door, creating a secluded environment that would allow their private conversation to unfold without any unwanted interruptions or eavesdropping. This deliberate action on Lorraine's part demonstrated a clear intent to shield their dialogue from external scrutiny. This enabled the two individuals to speak freely and candidly without concern for their words being overheard by others.

"OK, what's wrong?" Lorraine asked, concerned.

"OK, so not so long ago, someone turned up at my place. My Ex, Karen."

"Okay, and?"

"She's claiming that I have... well, I have a child."

"Do you?"

"I've no idea. I mean, if I did, she didn't tell me, and it's been about five years since I last saw her."

"First, you need to know for definite that you do have a child, and that it's actually yours."

"My thoughts as well. Not only that, she cheated on me with someone else, at the time."

"Oh, I see. How did you find out?"

"I caught her with him in my bed."

"Damn, that's harsh. OK, first you need a DNA test performed, because it seems she can't be trusted. Did she say what she wanted?"

"Yes, she thinks, and she's deluded with her thoughts. She thinks that she can come back into my life and we will just play happy families. It isn't going to happen."

Maxine swiftly emerged from the interior with the requested beverages in hand. With a sense of purpose, she promptly delivered the drinks and then decisively closed the patio door, sealing off the outdoor area. Her actions were marked by a brisk, no-nonsense demeanour, indicating a high degree of competence and attentiveness in her role.

"I'm glad you came and told me straight away. It means a lot to me, Steve."

McMatters gently leaned in, his heart swelling with emotion as he placed a tender kiss on Lorraine's lips. In that simple yet powerful gesture, a world of unspoken understanding passed between them. Lorraine's compassionate and nurturing demeanour, especially in the face of such a delicate situation, was truly refreshing. It served as a soothing balm amidst what could have easily spiralled into chaos and emotional turmoil. Her ability to confront the matter with a level head and an unwaveringly caring touch spoke volumes about her empathetic nature, a quality that stood in stark contrast to the heightened emotions or impulsive reactions that others might have succumbed to under similar circumstances.

Lorraine's calm composure shone like a beacon of light in the darkness, creating an atmosphere imbued with comfort and trust. It allowed both to breathe deeply, letting go of the tension while inviting vulnerability into their exchange. Each word spoken between them felt gentle; each silence embraced rather than feared. This exceptional sensitivity from Lorraine, not only helped ease McMatters' worries, but also fostered an environment where they could both navigate their feelings without the weight of anxiety pressing down upon them. In this intimate moment, relief washed over them like warm sunlight breaking through heavy clouds, illuminating their connection and infusing it with hope for what lay ahead. The simple act of sharing this space together, became not just a momentary reprieve, but rather the foundation upon which deeper understanding and healing could begin to blossom beautifully between them.

"Let's see what the DNA test results reveal and proceed from there."

"Jarvis is getting me some intel and arranging the DNA test."

"Good."

Lorraine was increasingly convinced that she needed to take a firm and unwavering stance with Karen, as the situation weighed heavily on her mind. She found herself grappling with a whirlwind of emotions, unable to comprehend why it had taken Karen an astonishing five years to inform McMatters about the existence of a child. This revelation struck Lorraine as not only highly unusual, but also deeply puzzling, leaving her feeling unsettled and suspicious. After all, one would naturally expect someone in Karen's position, who was aware of such significant news to reach out much sooner than this, particularly when it came to acknowledging the existence of a child, whom McMatters seemed completely unaware of. The prolonged delay in Karen's disclosure only served to heighten Lorraine's bewilderment and unease. It felt as if there were layers upon layers of unspoken truths lurking beneath the surface. With each passing day, Lorraine felt an increasing urgency to assert herself in this matter; she recognized that she could no longer remain passive or uncertain. The need to lay down the law and clearly communicate her feelings had become imperative, if she hoped to get to the bottom of this perplexing and concerning development. In doing so, she aimed not just for clarity, but also for understanding. An opportunity for both women to confront their emotions surrounding this unexpected twist in their lives with honesty and compassion.

Chapter Eleven
The Club

Jarvis, was diligently working in his office, having sent some of his trusted associates out to begin investigating the claims made by Karen. As Jarvis was focused on the task at hand, his colleague McMatters entered the office, accompanied by Lorraine.

"Good morning, Jarvis," said Lorraine.

Lorraine brewed a fresh pot of coffee, the rich aroma filling the entire office, and settled down at her desk. She ready to dive into preparations for the exciting evening festivities ahead. As the gracious host of tonight's gathering, she was acutely aware that there were several essential tasks awaiting her attention. Each one vital to ensure everything was impeccably arranged for the guests who would soon arrive. With a deep breath and a heart full of anticipation, Lorraine methodically reviewed her checklist. She was carefully laying out all the necessary items, while making final adjustments to create an inviting and delightful atmosphere for everyone who would be joining her. Meanwhile, McMatters took a moment to check in on some of his nightclub staff members, as he understood how crucial it was to maintain morale during these bustling times. As an owner of the club, he felt deeply responsible for ensuring not only the smooth operation of his establishment, but also the well-being of each team member who contributed so much to its success. By personally connecting with his staff and offering words of encouragement, or simply listening to their concerns, McMatters demonstrated his unwavering commitment to cultivating a positive and attentive working environment. He recognized that amidst potential complexities and stresses inherent in their fast-paced industry, fostering strong relationships could make all the difference. Back at her desk, Lorraine made every effort possible; she sought answers from Jarvis about any last-minute details that needed addressing or adjustments that could further enhance their guests' experience. She appreciated Jarvis's insights, as his knowledge often proved invaluable in transforming her gatherings into memorable occasions filled with warmth and joy.

"So, what's the score with this Karen?" Lorraine asked.

"She broke him, Lorraine. They had been in a relationship for a few years. She cheated on him, and stole five thousand pounds. He hasn't fully recovered from the betrayal."

"Makes sense."

"She's a piece of work though, coming back and doing this."

Lorraine felt a sense of worry and apprehension, but she remained confident that by working together with the others involved, they would be able to find a solution and get the situation sorted out. Despite the concern she was experiencing, Lorraine's belief in their collective ability to address the issue constructively provided her with a reassuring sense of optimism. Lorraine was eager to reconnect with the Blythe's, as she was aware that this day held significant importance for their family. She knew she needed to make time to catch up with them and learn more about the important events or milestones they were experiencing. Lorraine was attentive to the Blythe's' lives and wanted to show her support and interest in what was transpiring in their world on this momentous occasion.

"Blythe, good afternoon. How's it going?" asked Lorraine.

"Not too bad so far. The first shipment is in, and my guys are currently processing it. We are just waiting for the second shipment, which should arrive early this evening," replied Blythe.

"Do you need anything?"

"No, we are all good. It should go smoothly."

"Okay, we can talk later, Blythe," said Lorraine.

"Okay bye Lorraine," said Blythe. Lorraine felt a sense of relief as she hung up the phone, reassured that everything was proceeding smoothly.

As the compassionate manager of the operation, her primary responsibility revolved around the crucial task of periodically checking in with her team. This routine was not merely a formality; it was an opportunity for her to connect with each member. She could understand their challenges and triumphs on a personal level, and to ensure that the day-to-day activities were unfolding according to plan. By engaging in these thoughtful check-ins, she could maintain an overarching oversight of the operations while fostering a supportive environment, where open communication thrived. Moreover, this proactive approach enabled her to swiftly identify and address any potential issues that might arise, before they could escalate into significant problems. Whether it was a minor hiccup or a more pressing concern, she made it a priority to tackle these challenges head-on. Her unwavering commitment to keeping the operation running efficiently and effectively, not only ensured a smooth workflow, but also cultivated a sense of trust and collaboration within her team. With every interaction, she reinforced the idea that each person's contributions were valued, creating an atmosphere where everyone felt empowered to succeed together.

"Have you got to grips with the Blythe's now, Lorraine?" asked Jarvis.

"Yes, they seem to be getting organized after what happened. Now, I'm trying to work out if they need more men. They lost a lot when they attacked here, so my main concern is whether they're covering everything okay," Lorraine replied.

"Understandable. If they need more men, let me know."

"Will do."

Lorraine made her way downstairs, descending the steps to the lower level of the building where she intended to meet with Paulie and McMatters.
"Hi guys." McMatters greeted Lorraine with a gentle kiss. The two had developed a close relationship, and their interactions were often marked by affection and familiarity. I have an idea for two cocktails," said Lorraine, her eyes sparkling with excitement. She enjoyed experimenting with different flavour combinations and taking pride in her mixology skills.

"Sounds good," replied McMatters, nodding in approval. "I know you're quite skilled when it comes to making delightful cocktail choices." He valued Lorraine's expertise in this area and was eager to see what creative concoctions she had in mind.

"We have the general Margaritas but I'm thinking of a change in flavour, like adding a Mango Margarita."

Paulie, the experienced bartender, moved purposefully around the bar, carefully surveying the available ingredients and supplies. He was ensuring that the establishment had all the necessary components to prepare the requested cocktail. As a skilled mixologist, Paulie knew the importance of having the right tools and ingredients on hand to craft the perfect drink for the customer upon request. His attentive inspection of the bar allowed him to quickly identify any missing items or shortages, enabling him to efficiently gather the required materials and begin the cocktail-making process.

"I will put in an order for what I'm missing, Lorraine," said Paulie.

"Thanks, Paulie. The other is a new cocktail. Let's call it a signature cocktail; no one anywhere has this recipe," Lorraine replied.

"That sounds fantastic, Lorraine," said McMatters.

"You will need lemonade, Russian Vodka, Peach Schnapps, Midori, and Blue Curacao," said Lorraine.

"That sounds interesting," Paulie said, writing the recipe down.

"Once you've got the ingredients, let me know. I'll show you how 'Slimer' is put together," Lorraine added.

"Will do, and I can't wait to try it," said Paulie.

"We've got a Stag-do in tonight, Paulie. So, it might get lively," said McMatters.

"That will be fun. I'll get James to help out down here and put Tommy upstairs if you're okay with it."

"All good, Paulie," said McMatters.

Lorraine and McMatters, the pivotal figures in the business, made their way back to the upstairs office. They would diligently tackle a myriad of administrative and managerial tasks that are essential for the smooth running of their establishment. Their commitment to ensuring everything operates seamlessly reflects not only their dedication to the business, but also to their employees and patrons alike. Meanwhile, down on the bustling floor, Paulie, the devoted bar operations manager, took charge of coordinating and overseeing his team of enthusiastic bar staff. With a keen eye for detail and an innate ability to motivate others, Paulie ensured that his team were well-prepared and poised to deliver an efficient service to every patron who walked through the door. His leadership created a supportive atmosphere where each staff member felt valued, allowing them to provide exceptional experiences that kept customers returning time after time.

"Right, I'm off. I have a few errands to run. See you later," Lorraine said to Jarvis and McMatters.

Chapter Twelve
Lorraine's Place

Lorraine arrived home just as Maxine was putting the finishing touches on a freshly, prepared meal. The timing couldn't have been more perfect. As soon as she walked through the door, the enticing aroma wafted through the air, beckoning her to the kitchen for a delightful, soul-warming meal. Maxine greeted her with a warm smile and a hot meal. Lorraine eagerly recounted the latest drama filled events to her mum, Maxine. It seems that McMatters' ex Karen, has unexpectedly resurfaced, bearing the shocking news that he has a child, a revelation that has undoubtedly shaken up the status quo. Maxine listened intently, her eyes widening with each new scandalous detail that Lorraine divulged about this unexpected development in McMatters' personal life. The situation has all the makings of a spicy telenovela plot twist, leaving both women utterly captivated and desperate to discover how this perplexing scenario will ultimately unfold.

"If she thinks she's getting her claws stuck back into McMatters, then Karen is very much mistaken." Said Lorraine.

"Do you think you can stop her?" asked Maxine.

"Watch this space. She isn't pulling that shit."

Lorraine was absolutely fuming at the mere idea of her nemesis, Karen, rekindling her relationship with the notorious scoundrel, McMatters. The very thought of those two miscreants reuniting made Lorraine's blood boil with unbridled rage. She could scarcely contain her disdain as visions of Karen and McMatters frolicking off into the sunset together filled her mind, causing her to grind her teeth in sheer frustration. Lorraine was utterly appalled and determined to put a stop to this travesty before it was too late, no matter the cost. Her hatred for this potential coupling knew no bounds. Lorraine understood her boyfriend McMatters harboured a deep-seated animosity towards Karen, and for good reason.

The details of which had become the stuff of office legend. McMatters would visibly stiffen and his face would contort into an expression of pure disdain at the name Karen, as if he had just caught a whiff of spoiled mayonnaise. Lorraine couldn't help but chuckle inwardly whenever she witnessed these tell-tale signs, knowing full well the juicy backstory that fuelled McMatters' intense dislike of his ex. Lorraine hurriedly hopped into the shower, hastily threw on some clothes, and mulled over the recent happenings as she dried her damp locks. "That Karen, what a saucy minx!" Lorraine mused to herself, silently praying she could avoid an encounter with that cheeky little troublemaker anytime in the foreseeable future. Lorraine had no fear of facing off against Karen, oh no, not in the slightest.

In fact, the very thought of running into that troublesome woman made Lorraine's blood boil. If their paths were to cross, Lorraine knew she might just lose her cool and deck Karen right there and then. The mere prospect of having to deal with Karen's insufferable attitude and behaviour was enough to set Lorraine on edge, as she dreaded the possibility of being pushed to the point of physical retaliation. Lorraine was determined to avoid an altercation, but she couldn't help but fantasize about finally putting Karen in her place, should the opportunity present itself. In the blink of an eye, Lorraine had transformed herself into a vision of sartorial splendour, eagerly anticipating her night out at the exclusive club. With a flourish, she swiftly grabbed her phone and summoned her trusty chauffeur, commanding him to arrive post-haste and whisk her away to her destination of delight.

Chapter Thirteen
The Club

McMatters' was still loitering at the club, his brow
furrowed in a perplexed expression, when Lorraine
finally arrived on the scene. Apparently, he had been
standing there, scratching his head and muttering under
his breath, completely befuddled by the turn of events,
long after everyone else had departed for the evening.
Lorraine couldn't help but chuckle at the sight of her
hopelessly confused lover, wondering what on earth
could have left McMatters' so thoroughly flummoxed and
discombobulated. Seeing that they were finally alone for
a bit, Lorraine took the opportunity to try and keep her
companion thoroughly distracted. She playfully grabbed
his hand and led him away to the VIP section, knowing
full well that all the staff had already departed to get
ready for the evening's festivities.

Lorraine was well acquainted with the patterns around
here, so she figured they could enjoy a little private time
together. Once sequestered in the VIP area, she sat him
down on the plush, circular sofa with its high, discreet
backs. The setup was practically tailor made for engaging
in some clandestine activities, don't you think? Lorraine
had a mischievous glint in her eye as she considered all
the delightfully scandalous possibilities that this cosy
little nook presented. Lorraine straddled him, her legs on
either side of his body, and placed tender kisses along his
neck and ears. With a mischievous grin, she slowly
unzipped his pants, her nimble fingers gently caressing
and teasing his most sensitive areas. She could feel him
beginning to react to her playful ministrations, his body
responding eagerly to her touch. Once the situation
became intense, she recognized that she had him right
where she wanted him. Assuming a strategic position,
she proceeded to give him a vigorous, no holds barred

ride. She knew this was exactly what he needed. A thorough release to help him unwind and alleviate the built-up tension.

McMatters' had gone from a state of high stress and tension to one of intense, uncontrollable horniness. They were now consumed by a raging hormonal surge that threatened to disrupt the very fabric of the workplace.

The once professional atmosphere had been replaced by an electric, sexually charged energy, it was as if the building itself had been imbued with an intoxicating aphrodisiac. Now McMatters' was feeling quite at ease, a contented grin spreading across his face. He simply adored Lorraine, she always seemed to have an innate understanding of exactly what was required in any given situation. Her uncanny ability to intuitively grasp his needs, often before he could even articulate them himself, never failed to fill him with a deep sense of appreciation and affection. In her presence, McMatters could let go of any lingering tension or stress, secure in the knowledge that Lorraine would expertly navigate them through whatever challenges lay ahead. Later that evening the club opened, and it was a lively night as predicted.

Jarvis did a walk around the club making sure everyone was enjoying themselves while McMatters and Lorraine were in the office. Lorraine sat with her feet up at her desk while McMatters was pouring a drink from his decanter. A pair of hands slipped around McMatters' waist.

"Hey there sexy," said Karen.

McMatters spun around, his movements as erratic and uncoordinated as a newborn giraffe desperately trying to navigate its first steps on shaky legs. Each awkward twist and turn seemed to amplify the sense of chaos in the room, creating a scene both humorous and chaotic. As he flailed about in confusion, Karen blissfully oblivious to her surroundings saw her chance. With an impulsive enthusiasm that bordered on reckless, she lunged forward, attempting to pucker her lips for what she envisioned as a romantic yet clumsy kiss on McMatters' unsuspecting face. However, much like McMatters' own lack of spatial awareness, Karen's timing was utterly off. Instead of landing the affectionate peck she had hoped for, she ended up smushing her face against his shoulder with a comical squish.

The collision left behind an unmistakable mark, a big, sloppy imprint of bright lipstick smeared across his shirt collar, an unintended badge of embarrassment that was both amusing and cringe-worthy. At that moment of distraction and mishap, Lorraine came from behind the fray with fierce determination. Fuelled by a mix of indignation and protective instinct at witnessing this farcical display unfold before her eyes, Lorraine seized her opportunity to intervene decisively. In one swift motion that would make even the toughest boxer tip his cap in admiration, she landed a punch squarely on Karen's unsuspecting face with such force that it sent shockwaves through the room. The sheer impact reverberated through the air around them and sent Karen tumbling toward the ground with a resounding thud, a sound reminiscent of a sack of potatoes unceremoniously dropped from a great height. It was an unexpected end to what had started as an awkward encounter, but perfectly encapsulated the unpredictable nature of their interactions. Moments like these were woven into their shared experiences, a blend of laughter, chaos, and surprise that defined their tumultuous relationships.

Jarvis arrived just in the nick of time to witness an astonishing and delightfully unexpected turn of events: Lorraine, normally so reserved, reared back and landed a solid punch squarely on Karen's unsuspecting face. The impact sent Karen tumbling unceremoniously to the floor in a heap, leaving her utterly bewildered. Jarvis couldn't help but stifle a chuckle at the sheer absurdity of the situation unfolding before his eyes; it was as if he was watching a scene from an outrageous movie. He silently commended Lorraine's flair for the theatrical, marvelling at how someone who usually blended into the background had suddenly taken centre stage. Both Jarvis and McMatters stood utterly stunned as they witnessed this unexpected display of self-assuredness and sheer force from Lorraine.

Their eyes widened in disbelief as they realized that this unassuming woman was more than capable of handling herself, much to their astonishment. In another shocking turn of events, Lorraine swiftly seized hold of Karen's hair with surprising determination; it was almost as if she had tapped into some hidden reservoir of strength that none had anticipated. With remarkable resolve, she dragged Karen backwards towards the back door. Before either Jarvis or McMatters could fully process what was happening or even think to intervene, Lorraine had unceremoniously thrown Karen out through the exit with an air of finality that left them both slack-jawed in amazement at her audacious actions. It became abundantly clear that Lorraine was full of hidden depths, an unexpected warrior beneath her gentle exterior and would not easily be underestimated again. The ongoing astonishment etched on Jarvis and McMatters' faces spoke volumes about their newfound respect for her capabilities; what they witnessed that day would likely change how they viewed her forever.

"Drink darling?" mocked McMatters

Jarvis and McMatters were utterly overcome with uncontrollable laughter, their joyous mirth echoing through the room like music, creating a contagious atmosphere of light heartedness. The sheer absurdity of the moment had struck them both, igniting fits of giggles that seemed to have no end. Once the hilarity began to subside, McMatters, with a gleam of affection in his eyes, decided to offer a warm and affectionate embrace to Lorraine. He leaned in gently and planted a quick peck on her cheek a gesture filled with genuine warmth and camaraderie. Lorraine, caught off guard by this unexpected display of affection amidst the chaotic laughter, likely found the entire spectacle both bewildering and mildly disturbing. Her expression danced between confusion and amusement as she processed the whirlwind of emotions surrounding her; it was as if she was navigating an unfamiliar landscape filled with both joy and uncertainty, leaving her wondering how such laughter could transform into such heartfelt kindness in an instant.

"That infuriating woman has some nerve. Next time, I'll batter her."

"I didn't know you could handle yourself like that." said Jarvis.

"I learned that a long time ago, it was part of survival back then," said Lorraine."

Jarvis passed McMatters and Lorraine a drink.
"Here's to taking out the trash!" They all clinked glasses in unison.

McMatters' found himself pondering deeply about Lorraine's past, a tapestry woven with both known facts and the shadows of untold stories. While he was familiar with the main details of her life, he lacked insight into the full extent of the challenges and adversities she had faced throughout her journey. It intrigued him to consider that, despite her seemingly composed exterior, there was likely a wealth of experience hidden beneath the surface. These experiences that had forged her resilience and shaped her character. The recent display of Lorraine's negotiation skills during their interaction with Blythe had revealed a formidable side to her personality. It raised questions in McMatters' mind: What other talents lay dormant within her? What depths of capability had she yet to unveil? As he reflected on these possibilities, he couldn't help but wonder how far she had been pushed in life before arriving at this moment, what trials and tribulations had tested her mettle? Each thought led him down a path of curiosity, seeking to understand not just who Lorraine was now, but also who she might have been before circumstance polished her into the skilled individual standing before him today. The more McMatters' observed Lorraine, the deeper his feelings grew; it was as if each fleeting glance revealed another layer of her complexity and charm. The way she moved through life, with a blend of grace and vulnerability, captivated him in ways he had never anticipated. It ignited a profound desire within him not just to be by her side but to shield her from the world's harsh realities. Each smile she offered seemed to illuminate the dim corners of his heart, while every shadow that crossed her path stirred an instinctual urge within him to safeguard her from any harm that might come her way. This burgeoning connection left him contemplating not only his own emotions, but also the lengths he would go to ensure she felt cherished and secure in an often-unpredictable world.

Chapter Fourteen
Lorraine's Place

Lorraine stumbled through the front door the next morning, bleary-eyed and dishevelled after a long night of revelry at the nightclub followed by a night at McMatters' place. The clock struck a shameful ten am, and Lorraine knew she was in dire need of a wardrobe refresh before attempting to show her face at the club again. Her current ensemble, which included last night's makeup and a skirt that may or may not have been on backwards, simply wouldn't cut it. Lorraine sighed, already dreading the task of finding a presentable outfit that didn't reek of stale cocktails and questionable decisions. But alas, the show must go on. It was time to rally, freshen up, and head back out into the nightclub where Lorraine has some work to catch up on.

"Hi, Mum! Can't stop too long, but how did the date go?"

"Oh, Lorraine, it was wonderful! You should have seen it!"

"As long as you enjoyed yourself, that's all that matters."

"Oh, I did. Demetrio was a perfect gentleman."

"I bet he was!"

"Whose mind is in the gutter now?"

"So, will you see Demetrio again, Mum?"
"I hope so!"

"OK, I need to jump in the shower, change, and get back out. Busy bee!"

"You should eat, Lorraine."

"I will, but it will be on the move today."

Lorraine rushed upstairs, her heart racing with a delightful mix of heat and anticipation that coursed through her veins. Wasting no time, she quickly shed her clothing, the fabric pooling at her feet like fallen leaves in autumn. She eagerly stepped into the steamy, inviting embrace of the shower. The hot water cascaded over her skin in soothing rivulets, providing a cleansing sensation that felt like a warm hug, washing away the burdens and stresses of the day. Each droplet seemed to carry away worries as she inhaled deeply, filling her lungs with the refreshing scent of clean air mingled with steam. Lorraine relished this sacred moment—a private sanctuary where she could indulge in self-care and rejuvenation a cherished ritual that allowed her to reconnect with herself.

Feeling thoroughly revitalized and ready to face whatever challenges lay ahead, Lorraine carefully selected her ensemble for the day: a stylish grey suit that exuded professionalism yet carried an air of sophistication. She paired it with sleek black shoes that clicked confidently against the floor and a matching handbag that completed her polished look. Determined to present herself at her best, she meticulously styled her hair until it gleamed with a soft, lustrous shine reminiscent of sunlit silk. Her look was polished to perfection; each detail thoughtfully considered. As an artist prepares for their canvas, Lorraine swiftly applied makeup designed not just to enhance but also to empower. Every stroke was intentional as she ensured she was camera-ready for both professional engagements and unexpected opportunities alike. One last glance in the mirror filled her with self-assurance and pride at what she saw reflecting at her, an embodiment of strength. She dashed downstairs, eager and invigorated, ready to take on the day ahead with grace and determination.

"Okay, bye, Mum!" Lorraine shouted as she was halfway out of the door.

The Office

Lorraine's arrival at the club was fashionably late, a delightful spectacle that occurred just around one o'clock in the afternoon. As she strolled in, her presence was as vivid and vibrant as a burst of sunlight breaking through a cloudy sky. With her signature flair, she radiated warmth and joy, cheerfully greeting the staff with genuine enthusiasm that lifted their spirits. Swaying gracefully toward the office, Lorraine seemed poised to bestow upon the establishment not just her captivating presence but also her sharp wit; a combination that made every interaction feel like a breath of fresh air. The staff could hardly contain their excitement; they perked up like flowers turning toward the sun, eagerly anticipating the energy and entertainment Lorraine would bring to their workday. It was as though she carried an invisible spark with her, igniting inspiration and camaraderie among those lucky enough to be in her orbit. With each step she took, conversations transformed into laughter, mundane tasks turned into enjoyable challenges, and even the most routine aspects of work felt infused with newfound purpose under Lorraine's uplifting influence.

"Good morning, Lorraine," said Jarvis.

"Hi, lovely. You're looking good today," Steve greeted Lorraine.

"Morning, Steve," Lorraine greeted him, planting a quick peck on his cheek. "And good morning to you too, Jarvis." She shuffled over to the coffee pot, her shoes making a clicking sound against the tile floor.

"Alright, let's get this party started," she murmured, reaching for her favourite oversized mug.

"I'll be heading out shortly," said McMatters with a mischievous grin. "Got a little meeting lined up with one of our suppliers, you know, to discuss the, uh, liquid refreshments." He winked conspiratorially, already mentally preparing for a delightful afternoon of wheeling and dealing in the shadier side of the business world. McMatters was never one to let a chance for a cheeky tipple slip through his fingers, especially when it came at the expense of the company coffers.

"Sounds like a good time!" Lorraine exclaimed with a chuckle. "I simply must make time to connect with dear old Blythe today - nothing too dreadful, I'm sure."

"Catch you later," McMatters waved, walking out of the door.

Jarvis, the ever-reliable office jack of all trades, scurried out of the office, his to do list overflowing with a bizarre array of tasks to coordinate with the staff. Meanwhile, Lorraine, sipping her coffee, eyed her cup with a puzzled expression, as if it had somehow developed an unexplained hole, causing her beloved caffeine elixir to unceremoniously dribble down her chin.

Lorraine let out a heavy sigh as she eyed the phone, mentally preparing herself for the impending task. "Time to ring Blythe," she thought, her lips pursing in reluctance. Lorraine wasn't exactly accustomed to this whole "work" thing. It was a foreign and rather exhausting concept to her. Nevertheless, she took a deep breath and mustered the courage to make the call, bracing herself for the arduous endeavour that lay ahead.

"Blythe, how are things going?"

"Not good, Lorraine. I've been run off my feet, and quite frankly, I need more men. The second shipment was hijacked; the guys on the run were badly beaten. I've been trying to find out who did it. It's taken me all night and this morning to find out."

"OK, Blythe. More men I can sort, so who did it? Tell me all you can, one sec while I grab Jarvis."
Lorraine goes to the office door and whistles to get Jarvis's attention, which works like a charm. He comes up, and Lorraine closes the door.

"OK, Blythe. I've got Jarvis here. Tell us all from the start, please?"

"The first shipment went to plan, but the second, which was due in this afternoon, was hijacked. My men who were doing the run were badly beaten. They took the lot. I... I can't do anything. I've not enough men. It has taken me from when it happened until an hour ago to get the name of who did it."

"OK, who was it, Blythe?" said Jarvis.

"The Slaters. I've never heard of them, nor has anyone I know. It's puzzling."

"I will find out and sort it, Blythe. Between me and Lorraine, we will sort it out. Okay, so your guys are in hospital?"

"Yes, both of them." Said Blythe.

"Okay Blythe. Now, you normally run your side, and we don't get involved, but have the families of the guys who were attacked been sent care packs?" asked Jarvis.

"I normally would, but I'm down so many men. We're not pulling in enough now. That's why these two shipments are so important."

"Don't worry, we look after our own. I will get care packs sent out. Message me the details. I will get some more men for you. How's thirty? I know you're not down that many, but if this has happened once, it might happen again," said Jarvis.

"You can spare thirty men?" asked Blythe.

"I have many to hand anytime they're needed. Plus, if I get my hands on the Slaters, all of the families will be there as one."

"I wish I had done things differently." said Blythe.

"It's in the past. Now, your income is taking a hit. If you start to struggle, we can work something out." said Jarvis.

"Thank you. Really, Thank you."

"Blythe, I will contact you soon," said Lorraine.

Once the call had finally drawn to a close, both Lorraine and Jarvis exhaled deeply, releasing long-held breaths that seemed to carry away the tension of the moment. The exasperated sigh that escaped their lips was a testament to the emotional and mental toll of the conversation they had just endured. It was as if time stood still for a brief instance, allowing them to pause and fully process the sheer magnitude and intensity of what had transpired during those arduous minutes. The weight of their discussion lingered heavily in the air around them, an invisible shroud that mirrored their shared sense of fatigue and contemplation. Each word exchanged during that call echoed in their minds, reverberating with implications that felt almost overwhelming. In this moment of quiet reflection, they took a collective breath, granting themselves permission to mentally regroup and recover from this exhausting ordeal. It was not just a conversation; it was an emotional journey filled with raw vulnerability and complex feelings that demanded acknowledgment before moving forward.

"OK, Lorraine. As you're in training, that means you're with me. Do you think you're up for what might need to be done?" Asked Jarvis.

"When I said I'd take over the main management of the Blythes, I knew at some point I might need to get my hands dirty. It's not like I haven't done stuff like this before; it's more a case of not having to go all the way. But I'm good at showing whose boss." said Lorraine.

"At any point you don't think that you can go all the way, let me know. But for now, we have to do some digging and find the Slaters." said Jarvis.

Lorraine, in her usual enthusiastic fashion, scurried about the office with an infectious energy, determined to unravel the mystery that had everyone on edge. Her eyes sparkled with curiosity as she cornered each staff member, eager to gather any potential clues about the elusive Slaters. With each conversation, she drew out anecdotes and whispers, hoping to piece together the puzzle that seemed to grow more intricate by the minute. Meanwhile, after checking in with the club staff and gathering their insights, Jarvis made a strategic decision to reach out to the other two families that he strongly believed could hold critical information: the Bennetts and the Santos. These families were known for their connections and knowledge of all local happenings; Jarvis was convinced they could hold the key that would unlock this perplexing enigma. Leaving no stone unturned in his quest for answers, Jarvis reached out to everyone on the company payroll. He dialled number after number with a sense of urgency and hopefulness, desperately hoping that someone could shed light on this increasingly bizarre situation that had enveloped them all like a thick fog of confusion.

The office buzzed with an electronic hum, the sound of Lorraine's rapid-fire questioning intermingled with Jarvis's calls, which reverberated through the air as he hunted for answers like a bloodhound hot on a scent trail. It was all rather amusing, a chaotic symphony of inquiry if you weren't directly caught in its crosshairs. Within just an hour of his relentless pursuit for information, the men whom Jarvis had called began arriving at the club one by one. Paulie sprang into action almost immediately upon their entrance; his natural flair for hospitality ensured everyone was promptly served drinks as laughter filled the room. Meanwhile, Lorraine and Jarvis took it upon themselves to bring their guests up to speed regarding all that they knew about the Blythes and their dubious operations which seemed shrouded in shadows. Once Jarvis had finished laying out all the pertinent details, his voice steady but tinged with excitement, Lorraine turned towards her audience with a mischievous twinkle dancing in her eye. She leaned forward slightly and requested earnestly yet playfully that they put their ears to the ground like seasoned detectives sniffing out any juicy intel regarding the Slaters, a call to arms disguised as camaraderie among friends who shared this unexpected adventure together.

"Guys, one last thing: we will be issuing a reward for the Slaters' intel. The more we get, the better. Location, addresses, base of operations, what they deal in, where they come from this list could go on and on. How much impacts upon the amount of the reward," said Lorraine.

"Okay, let's get over to the Blythe's," directed Jarvis.

Jarvis gave a slight nod in Lorraine's direction, a subtle yet powerful gesture that served as his nonverbal endorsement of her impressive ability to manage the group of men she was working with. This small but significant movement, a gentle tilt of his head combined with his look, effectively conveyed his recognition and admiration for Lorraine's skilful handling of what could have been a challenging situation. It was as if he understood the nuances of her role, acknowledging not just her leadership but also the empathy and tact she employed to guide her team towards success. In a world where words often overshadow actions, Jarvis's minimalist form of acknowledgment spoke volumes. His quiet appreciation resonated deeply, letting Lorraine know that her efforts had not only met with his high standards, but had also left a lasting impression on him. This tacit approval, delivered in Jarvis's typically reserved yet thoughtful manner, highlighted the bond they shared a mutual respect forged through their professional interactions. After all Lorraine was still learning.

Lorraine

Lorraine felt as if she were practically vibrating with nerves, both externally and internally, as she found herself unexpectedly thrust into the gritty, shadowy world of her new job. In stark contrast to her previous cushy existence where the most stressful decision had been what flavour of coffee to order, this new reality was nothing short of overwhelming.

"Now this is what I call a rush," thought Lorraine, feeling the adrenaline coursing through her body like a powerful river, invigorating yet terrifying all at the same time. The unfamiliar underworld work environment surrounded her with an air of tension; it was alive with shadows that danced along the walls and whispers that seeped into every corner. Shady characters lurked in dimly lit nooks, exchanging glances filled with secrets and dubious dealings that sent shivers down her spine. Each figure seemed cloaked in mystery and danger, amplifying Lorraine's sense of dread as she stood there trembling like a leaf caught in a storm.

She felt utterly out of her element, as if she had stepped onto a stage where everyone else knew their lines except for her. The vibrant chaos around her was both exhilarating and frightening, a stark reminder that life could change in an instant. Lorraine realised all the years she had been chasing the adrenaline rush when she was stealing diamonds, that now she had a new rush to contend with and Lorraine was enjoying every minute of it.

Gone were the days of her cosy sparkling diamonds, instead, she found herself immersed in a realm that challenged her sensibilities at every turn, leaving her woefully unprepared for the realities of this new, decidedly less glamorous career path. Lorraine tried her best to appear calm and collected, but the reality was that she was a nervous wreck on the inside. Her hands trembled uncontrollably, and she could feel beads of sweat forming on her brow. She desperately hoped that no one would pick up on her obvious state of anxiety.

Lorraine silently prayed that she could get through the situation without completely embarrassing herself or giving away just how utterly terrified she was at that moment. Lorraine was a veritable rollercoaster of emotions as she embarked on this new chapter of her life. On one hand, she was positively giddy with anticipation, like a kid in a candy store let loose after hours. But on the other, the butterflies in her stomach were doing Olympic level gymnastics, reminding her that she was diving headfirst into the murky depths of the criminal underbelly. This was a world she had only ever glimpsed from the safety of her couch while binge watching true crime documentaries. Lorraine had hoped that she'd have had a little more time to mentally prepare, or maybe read the instruction manual before plunging into the unknown, but alas, fate had other plans. All she could do now was strap in, hold on tight, and pray she wouldn't end up in a body bag by the end of the week.

Jarvis was the epitome of organization and efficiency, a veritable machine when it came to navigating the intricate web of the city's various crime families. Lorraine couldn't help but feel a mixture of admiration and trepidation as she shadowed this seasoned pro, knowing full well that she had a lot to learn from him. However, the thought of potentially crossing paths with the Slaters loomed large in the back of Lorraine's mind. She couldn't help but wonder what kind of havoc those unpredictable scoundrels might unleash, and how on earth she would handle such a confrontation. One thing was certain... if she ever found herself staring down the Slaters, it would undoubtedly be a life altering experience, for better or for worse.

Lorraine steeled herself, summoning all her courage, fully aware that with Jarvis as her mentor, she might just find a way to navigate through the challenges that lay ahead. Despite this reassuring thought, a hint of dread crept into her heart at the prospect of the unknown ordeal awaiting her. Nonetheless, an undeniable excitement bubbled within her as she eagerly anticipated the chance to converse with Mr. McMatters. Her face lit up with a mischievous grin that danced in her eyes as she mentally rehearsed all the juiciest titbits, and intriguing anecdotes she simply had to share during their discussion. This conversation with McMatters was not merely an obligation; it represented a beacon of hope a vital opportunity that could illuminate her path through what felt like uncharted territory.

Lorraine longed for his insights and guidance, believing that his seasoned perspective would offer clarity amidst the fog of uncertainty. Each potential snippet of gossip or shared wisdom filled her mind like sparkling confetti. It inspired a sense of camaraderie and connection that she desperately hoped would help bridge any gaps in understanding or experience. With each moment ticking closer to their meeting, Lorraine's anticipation grew stronger. It was not just about surviving this ordeal but thriving through it with newfound knowledge and support by her side.

Chapter fifteen
Intel

Jarvis was pondering why Karen did not comply with the DNA test, which puzzled Jarvis. He found it perplexing that someone would claim to have a child with another individual but then refuse to undergo a paternity test to definitively establish their parental relationship. Jarvis was baffled by Karen's reluctance to provide conclusive proof of her assertion, as a paternity test would have offered a clear and objective means of verifying her claim. The lack of willingness to take such a straightforward step left Jarvis questioning the legitimacy of Karen's statement and wondering about her true motivations for making an unsubstantiated declaration. Jarvis found himself in a state of profound uncertainty, grappling with more questions than definitive answers regarding the situation.

Driven by this sense of ambiguity, Jarvis had decided to have Karen discreetly followed and monitored over the course of several weeks. During this period of surveillance, the investigators did not once observe Karen in the company of a child, nor did they identify any other individuals residing at the property in question. Based on this lack of evidence, the only reasonable conclusion that could be drawn was that there was no child, no pregnancy, and that Karen's previous claims were likely fabricated as a means of manipulating the situation and reintroducing McMatters back into her life. McMatters is likely to be outraged and furious in response to this development, and Lorraine may escalate the situation even further than just physically dragging Karen out by her hair. Jarvis then found himself pondering just how far Lorraine might be willing to go in this confrontation.

"Lorraine?"

"Yes, Jarvis."

"I have an update on Karen."

"Oh, aye."

"Do you know when Steve is back?"

"He should be here in the next ten minutes. I spoke to him not long ago."

"Good. I'll update you both at the same time, upon his return."

McMatters

McMatters strode into the office, and Lorraine and Jarvis immediately looked like they were bursting at the seams with things to share with him. It wasn't as if he'd been gone for an eternity, but apparently, in his brief absence, the office had descended into a veritable whirlwind of activity and gossip.

"OK, what's up?" asked McMatters.

"Perceptive as usual, Steve." said Jarvis.

"Where do we start, Jarvis?" asked Lorraine.

"I think Blythe's first, then Karen. You start off, Lorraine." said Jarvis.

"Thanks, Jarvis! Okay... after a call with Blythe this morning, it appears that he's had trouble with one of yesterday's shipments. The morning shipment had no issues, but the afternoon is another story. It was hijacked. Apparently, Blythe spent all that night and next morning trying to find out who it was." said Lorraine.

"Who was it?" asked McMatters.

"The Slaters," said Lorraine.

"Who the bloody hell are the Slaters?" asked McMatters.

"We have all of the teams out trying to answer the same question. The families have also been asked to find out who the Slaters are as well," said Jarvis.

"How did it happen?"

"Two of Blythe's guys were jumped and beaten badly. Apparently, as he's already down a lot of men, he was stretched too thin. To make matters worse, he isn't bringing in enough money to cover expenses, and those shipments were needed." said Lorraine.

"I'm going over shortly with Lorraine; we have thirty men on lend to Blythe while he gets himself sorted. If word gets out that he can't stop a shipment from getting hijacked then more will test his weakness," said Jarvis.

"Oh yes, you know they will" said McMatters.

McMatters poured himself a stiff drink, the rich amber liquid glinting in the soft light of the room and leaned back in his chair with a weary sigh. He was trying to make sense of the whirlwind of activity that had consumed their lives lately, a dizzying series of events that seemed to be spiralling out of control. It felt as though they had been trapped on a relentless hamster wheel, each turn bringing yet another crisis that clamoured for their immediate attention. This constant barrage left them with barely enough time to catch their breath, let alone reflect on what was happening around them.

As he swirled the drink in his glass, watching it catch the light like fleeting moments of clarity amid chaos, McMatters couldn't help but chuckle at the absurdity of it all. It was almost laughable how life had thrown one curveball after another each dilemma more perplexing than the last challenging their resilience and testing their limits. Yet amidst this pandemonium, there lingered a sense of camaraderie and shared experience; they were navigating this storm together. In that moment, he realized that sometimes laughter was needed as much as resolve to get through these turbulent times.

"Lorraine, are you up for all this? It might get a bit messy dealing with Blythe's situation," asked McMatters.

"I'm good. Jarvis will be with me, showing me how he does things and how he handles the family," said Lorraine.

"Don't worry, I will step in where needed, but I want Lorraine to lead with Blythe. She has shown him that she can handle things, but if there are any problems, I will be on hand with thirty men," Jarvis laughed.

"You said there was an update on Karen?" asked McMatters.

"Yes, interesting as well. She failed to turn up for the DNA testing which made me curious as to why. I have had Karen followed for the last few weeks. All if the time she was followed, not once has she been with a child. The guys had a look around where she is staying, and it is only her living there."

"So, she has lied about me having a child with her?"

"It seems so."

McMatters downed his drink, feeling the tumult of emotions swirling within him like a stormy sea. On one hand, he found himself captivated by the very idea of becoming a father. The thought of a tiny little child running around, gleefully calling him "Dad," filled his heart with warmth and longing. He could easily envision moments spent building forts out of blankets, teaching them to ride a bike for the first time, or sharing joyous laughter over silly bedtime stories. These cherished dreams tugged at his heartstrings in the most profound way. Yet, contrasting this sweet dream was an undeniable dread the realization that he absolutely did not want that child to be raised by Karen. The memory of her blatant lies still burned in his mind; it was a betrayal that stung deeply and left him feeling vulnerable and betrayed. Her outrageous outburst at the club only added fuel to his frustration, making it clear how ill-suited she was for such an important role as motherhood. How had he found himself entangled in such a complicated web of emotions? With each passing moment, McMatters felt more overwhelmed by this predicament that seemed to have appeared out of nowhere. He let out a heavy sigh as he pondered these conflicting feelings, hoping for clarity amidst the chaos that was swirling in his mind. Taking another swig from his glass in a desperate attempt to drown those tumultuous thoughts, he hoped that perhaps this liquid courage would provide some insight or at least numb the emotional pain just enough to think rationally about the situation ahead.

Just then, Lorraine noticed McMatters' distress and approached him with empathy radiating from her presence. Sensing the weight on his shoulders, she leaned in gently and placed a comforting kiss on his cheek before pouring him another drink with tender care. Her unwavering support reminded him that even amidst confusion and turmoil, there were still moments of kindness and understanding, elements vital for navigating through life's challenges together.

"Wait till I see her," said McMatters.

"Steve, we're off to see Blythe now, but we'll talk about this when I'm back, okay?"

Chapter Sixteen
Maxine

Maxine was positively giddy, dancing and prancing around her humble abode while belting out a joyful tune. For once in her life, this usually dour and dreary woman was brimming with unbridled excitement. Demetrio, the object of her affections, was finally gracing Lorraine's doorstep with his presence. Rather than the nervous wreck she might have been expected to become, Maxine was practically vibrating with delight at the prospect of playing host to her long-time crush. Her neighbours likely thought the poor woman had taken leave of her senses, but Maxine couldn't have cared less. Today was her day, and she was determined to make the most of it, no matter how uncharacteristically gleeful it made her appear. Maxine had set her sights on whipping up a veritable culinary masterpiece for the evening. A homemade meal fit for the gods, followed by a decadent, mouth-watering baked creation that would have even the most seasoned pastry chefs swooning. She had worked tirelessly, pouring her heart and soul into every step of the preparation, but now that the hard work was behind her, Maxine could finally take a deep breath and allow herself a moment of well-deserved relaxation.

With the meal and dessert firmly under her command, she could kick back, put her feet up, and bask in the glory of her culinary prowess, secure in the knowledge that she had absolutely nailed it. Maxine had a couple of spare hours to kill before her date with Demetrio arrived. In a burst of celebratory energy, she spent that time belting out show tunes and busting out some enthusiastic dance moves while tidying up the kitchen. With the house sparkling and her spirits high, Maxine then indulged in a little well-deserved pampering to ensure she looked and felt her absolute best, eagerly anticipating the evening of fun and excitement that lay ahead. Bubble bath, perfectly manicured nails, hair expertly styled. Maxine had pulled out all the stops, donning one of Lorraine's fabulous outfits, complete with a tantalizing surprise underneath. She could barely contain her excitement, as she waited to unveil this jaw dropping ensemble for Demetrio. This was going to be an evening to remember, filled with luxury, indulgence, and a healthy dose of sultry anticipation.

Once Maxine has completed her initial preparations, she joyfully retrieves an exquisite collection of aromatic candles, each one carefully chosen for its enchanting fragrance. As she opens the box, she is immediately enveloped by the delightful infusion of warm vanilla and rich caramel wafting through the air, a scent that brings back cherished memories of cosy gatherings and laughter shared with loved ones. With a flourish that reflects her creative spirit, she scatters the candles strategically around the dining room and elegantly adorns the table, transforming the space into a warm and inviting sanctuary where guests will feel truly welcomed. Not one to rest on her laurels or let any moment go to waste, the ever-enterprising Maxine dashes up the stairs with an infectious enthusiasm. Her mind buzzes with ambitious plans as she envisions how to elevate every corner of her home with even more fragrant candles that will delight her guests' senses. Upon reaching her bedroom, she carefully selects additional candles infused with alluring scents of blooming rose and delicate sweet pea; their gentle fragrance fills the air with promises of serenity and romance. However, demonstrating both patience and wisdom in her preparations, Maxine wisely refrains from lighting them just yet. She decides to save that dramatic flourish for the big unveiling, a moment when all will be ready to reveal. It was not just a beautifully decorated space, but also an atmosphere brimming with warmth and love, that reflects her thoughtful care for those who enter it.

Chapter Seventeen
Blythe

As Jarvis and Lorraine arrived in the Blythe's' area, they were suddenly jolted by a powerful explosion that reverberated through the ground beneath them, shaking their very sense of security. The moment was charged with tension as they exchanged concerned glances, each feeling the heavy weight of uncertainty settle around them like a thick fog. The force of the blast not only rattled their vehicle, but also sent a palpable sense of unease rippling through the air, igniting an instinctive awareness that this was no ordinary occurrence. It lingered between them like an unspoken question: just how devastating could the aftermath of this explosion ultimately prove to be? The situation had taken an undeniably ominous turn, leaving both Jarvis and Lorraine acutely aware that they would need to brace themselves for the potential fallout. They will need to confront whatever challenges might lie ahead in the wake of this startling and potentially dangerous development.

With urgency driving his actions, Jarvis quickly pulls over to the curb, prompting a swift reaction from seven other vehicles that formed a line behind them. A visual testament to their shared concern. Almost immediately, a thick cloud of acrid black smoke began to billow into the sky, resembling dark tendrils reaching out into the atmosphere. It carried with it a noxious blend of burning fuel and scorched rubber that invaded Jarvis' senses. The stinging sensation at the back of his throat served as a harsh reminder of their precarious position and made it increasingly difficult for him to breathe steadily. This was clearly no mere inconvenience; they were confronting something far more dangerous than they had anticipated. Recognizing the urgency of their predicament, Jarvis understood that swift action was essential to assess what had gone wrong, and to mitigate any potential risks or hazards stemming from this catastrophic event. He stepped out of his vehicle with determination coursing through him, followed closely by drivers from each accompanying car, who also disembarked in unison. This coordinated action not only emphasized the seriousness of their situation, but also underscored an implicit understanding among all present, the need for everyone involved to be alert and ready to tackle whatever challenges lay ahead. Their simultaneous departure from their vehicles, highlighted not just individual bravery, but also collective responsibility in facing adversity together. The gravity of these circumstances fostered an atmosphere ripe for collaboration. It became clear that by pooling their efforts and resources, they stood a better chance against whatever obstacles awaited them on this turbulent path forward.

"Okay, team, it looks like there's trouble ahead in Blythe's direction. When we get there, pull up quickly and secure the area. One group will do a house check before we all go in. Another will secure the front, and another the back. Everyone else, fan out and secure the surrounding area."

All the teams cautiously got back into their vehicles, and proceeded the remainder of their journey at a much more measured, deliberate pace. Recognizing the potential hazards that lay ahead, they opted to exercise greater prudence, and vigilance as they continued their way, taking care to navigate the route carefully, and avoid any further incidents or complications. The group's newfound sense of unease prompted them to travel the final stretch of their trip in a more restrained and tentative manner, prioritizing safety over speed.

Upon their arrival, the scene was marked by the signs of a dramatic explosion, with thick plumes of smoke emanating from Blythe's vehicle. It was evident that the car had been deliberately targeted and blown up in a conspicuous manner, sending a clear and unmistakable message. This brazen act of destruction conveys a serious warning, one that the perpetrators will likely come to regret delivering, as the consequences of such a bold and dangerous statement could prove far-reaching and severe. Jarvis suspected that the recent disturbance was likely the work of the Slater family.

It was evident that the Slaters were determined to seize control, even if it meant resorting to forceful tactics. The situation had become increasingly tense, as the Slaters made it clear they were willing to use any means necessary to achieve their aims and cement their dominance over the region. Jarvis knew this posed a serious threat, and that the community would need to be vigilant, and prepared to respond to the Slaters aggressive posturing, and the potential for violence if they continued down this path of escalation. It was with a heavy heart that Jarvis reflected on the unfortunate situation facing the Slater family. He knew that the consequences they would now have to endure for their reckless actions were truly unfortunate and regrettable. Jarvis could not help but feel a sense of pity and sorrow for the difficult predicament the Slaters had now found themselves in due to their lapse in judgment. The looming punishment they were about to face, though warranted, was still a sobering and disheartening prospect, that Jarvis wished could have been avoided.

Jarvis and Lorraine stood at a respectful distance, their eyes fixed on Blythe, who was rooted at his doorway with an expression that conveyed a tumultuous blend of rage and deep anguish. The flames danced wildly around his car, crackling and consuming it in a fiery embrace that mirrored the turmoil within him. Lorraine's bodyguards remained vigilant nearby their senses heightened as they scanned the surroundings for any potential threats.

Meanwhile, the thirty men accompanying them moved with purpose and determination, quickly establishing a secure perimeter to protect everyone involved in this chaotic scene. As tension thickened in the air, Jarvis's men surged forward without so much as a glance back or an inquiry into Blythe's feelings; they barged past him and entered his home with an unsettling sense of urgency. Their disregard for Blythe's emotional state added another layer to the already charged atmosphere.

Standing silently beside Blythe, was another woman who seemed equally affected by the chaos unfolding before them. He turned to her with an intensity that demanded silence, a firm but gentle grip on her arm served as both reassurance and instruction, signalling her to remain quiet and still amid the storm of emotions swirling around them. In this moment of crisis, their lives intertwined in unexpected ways, revealing not just personal struggles, but also the fragility of human connection when faced with sudden disaster.

"Blythe I'm guessing this is their handy work?" asked Jarvis.

"Yep, it seems so," said Blythe.

"Blythe, you remember Lorraine. So, who's this lovely lady stood next to you?" asked Jarvis.

"Jarvis this is my sister Katrina Garcia. Katrina this is Jarvis," said Blythe.

Katrina cautiously extended her hand towards Jarvis, her heart fluttering with uncertainty as she pondered how he might respond to this intimate gesture. There was a delicate hesitation in the air, as if time itself had paused to observe their interaction. Jarvis, noticing her tentative approach, carefully grasped her hand with surprising gentleness and delicacy. Instead of merely executing a simple handshake, he took an unexpected step further by bringing her hand to his lips and placing a soft, tentative kiss upon it. This intimate act sent a ripple of emotions through Katrina; she felt both flattered and bewildered by the unexpected affection expressed through such a tender gesture. Yet, lingering doubts clouded her thoughts, as she was left grappling with the uncertainty surrounding Jarvis's true intentions, and the deeper implications of his actions. The atmosphere around them felt charged with an undercurrent of unspoken tension, imbued with layers of meaning that neither of them dared to voice aloud. Katrina found herself caught in a swirl of conflicting feelings. Was this kiss merely an act of polite formality as he had perhaps intended, or did it signify something far more profound? The ambiguity hung in the air like a heavy fog, obscuring clarity and leaving her wondering how deep their connection truly ran.

Meanwhile, Lorraine couldn't help but smirk knowingly as she observed Jarvis's captivated gaze, which was fixed intently on Katrina. She recognized that he was thoroughly enjoying the sight before him. The way Katrina's eyes sparkled with curiosity mixed with trepidation. And how despite his best efforts to maintain an air of neutrality, his interest was palpable. Lorraine's keen perception allowed her to see beyond Jarvis's composed exterior; she understood his true feelings, that lay just beneath the surface, like a hidden treasure waiting to be discovered. This insight granted Lorraine a sense of power and control over the unfolding situation; while Jarvis attempted to keep his demeanour unaffected as if nothing was amiss, she could see through his actions clearly. The subtle exchanges between them, became laden with unspoken communication. It was a dance between attraction and uncertainty that highlighted not only their individual desires, but also the intricate dynamics at play between these two individuals, who were caught in what felt like an emotional tug-of-war.

"We might as well go in" said Blythe, unsure if he liked Jarvis's attention towards his sister.

But he knew he couldn't do anything about it. He realized that if he tried, he wasn't sure which of them would swing for his head first.

As soon as Jarvis and Lorraine crossed the threshold into the house, they were immediately overwhelmed by a powerful, musky scent that assaulted their senses. The potent, pungent aroma seemed to permeate every corner of the space, hitting them full force and causing them to scrunch their noses in response. It was an intense, almost suffocating smell that was impossible to ignore, leaving them both taken aback by its sheer strength and pervasiveness the moment they entered the dwelling. The unpleasant stench, a combination of body odour and overpowering perfume, was overwhelming.

Lorraine struggled to maintain her composure, muttering to herself repeatedly, "Must not wrinkle nose, must not show it's knocking me sick, must hurry this visit." The foul smell was clearly distressing her, and she was determined to get through the unpleasant experience as quickly as possible. The house Lorraine noticed, was in a rather dilapidated state, evoking memories of the nineteen eighties era. The overall aesthetic was drab and unkempt, with a predominance of brown tones, with a general sense of grime and neglect pervading the property. The rundown condition of the house was immediately apparent to Lorraine, leaving her with an impression of a bygone time that had not aged well.

"Well, Blythe, as promised, thirty men are currently securing the house as we talk," said Lorraine.

"Thank you for all of this," Blythe replied.

"How are your men?" asked Jarvis.

"One is out of the hospital with a broken leg, two ribs, and a bruised wrist, but he's OK. The other must stay in for at least two more days. He has suffered a lot of broken bones, and it wasn't until he was in the hospital that they found he had been stabbed as well. Small blade, so not too bad." said Blythe.

"I'm going to need regular updates as we get closer to finding the Slaters. The situation is becoming more unpredictable." said Lorraine.

"The families are working overtime to get me intel. I've offered a reward on this, so spread the word. I want lots of intel on the Slaters," said Jarvis.

"Can someone shout to Tommy for me?" asked Blythe.

A young man entered the room, appearing somewhat stuck in a time warp, wearing a shell suit. He was also bashful and uneasy in the face of the evident power dynamics at play. His demeanour suggested a sense of trepidation and discomfort, as if he was intimidated or overwhelmed by the palpable authority and influence present within the dining room. The man's sheepish and hesitant body language conveyed a subtle acknowledgment of the formidable presence and control that permeated the environment, leaving him feeling humbled and cautious in his approach.

"Blythe" said Tommy.

"Ah good Tommy, can you get word to all our guys. Jarvis is offering a cash reward for any intel on the Slaters," said Blythe.

"Will do," said Tommy.

Tommy hastily departed to deliver the urgent message entrusted to him. Hurrying through the streets, he was acutely aware of the importance and time sensitive nature of the task at hand. Failure to swiftly convey the critical information could have serious consequences, so Tommy maintained a brisk pace, navigating the crowded urban environment with a keen sense of purpose and determination. The weight of the responsibility he had been entrusted with weighed heavily on his mind as he pressed onward, cognizant that any delay could jeopardize the success of the mission.

"We will speak soon, Blythe. Be careful. It's nice to meet you, Katrina. I hope that we will meet again soon," said Lorraine.

As Jarvis prepared to depart, a wave of mixed emotions washed over him, heightened by the weight of the moment. Katrina, with a furtive glance that spoke volumes about the intensity of their exchange, discreetly passed him a sealed note. Recognizing the unspoken message in her eyes, he felt a sense of responsibility settle upon his shoulders. He understood that this was no ordinary message. Exercising caution, and respecting the delicate nature of their situation, Jarvis resolved it would be wise not to open the note until he had left the premises. He was acutely aware that once he stepped outside, he would be enveloped in a different world, one far removed from potential prying eyes, or ears lurking within the house. In this moment of clarity, Jarvis grasped just how crucial it was to maintain his discretion, and to safeguard any confidential information entrusted to him. With deliberate care, he tucked the note securely away into his inside pocket, ensuring its safety amidst his other belongings, resolving to examine its contents later when he could find solace and privacy. A quiet park bench perhaps, or even his favourite coffee shop where familiarity wrapped around him like a comforting blanket. Jarvis felt an overwhelming sense of purpose. The anticipation swirled within him; what secrets did this note hold?

"I'm sure we will meet again, Katrina," said Jarvis.

He placed his hands on her shoulders, pulled her in, and gave her a kiss on the cheek. Jarvis then turned and shook Blythe's hand.
Jarvis and Lorraine, accompanied by Lorraine's security team, returned to their vehicle, while the rest of the group remained with the Blythe's to help them restore order in their family.

"Oh my, that house needs bulldozing and fumigation," said Lorraine.

"I can't get the smell out of my nose," said Jarvis.

Chapter Eighteen
The Office

McMatters was overjoyed and filled with a profound sense of relief, upon witnessing the return of Jarvis and Lorraine. As Lorraine was still new to the intricacies and challenges of this game they were playing, McMatters felt a deep, almost paternal instinct, to ensure her wellbeing and safeguard her from any potential harm. He was determined to use his experience and knowledge to shield Lorraine and make certain she navigated this unfamiliar terrain with the utmost care and security. McMatters' heart swelled with a fierce protectiveness, driven by a genuine desire to support and uplift his newfound companion, as she bravely ventured forth, placing his utmost priority on Lorraine's comfort and safety within this high-stakes environment.

"Welcome back. How did it go?" asked McMatters.

"It went very well, but Blythe has issues," said Lorraine. "Blythe's car went boom. Looks like the Slaters managed to get close enough to blow it up, right outside his front door."

"Good job he has extra security now."

"It wasn't the only thing smoking," Lorraine said, laughing.

"I don't know what you mean," said Jarvis. Now remembering the note, he pulled it from his pocket and opened it to find... a number and "Call me anytime. XX K"

"Jarvis got a love letter" said Lorraine winding Jarvis up.

"Oh, who from?" asked McMatters.

"Blythe's sister Katrina," said Lorraine poking the bear.

Jarvis leaned back in his chair, allowing himself to fully savour the smooth, warm burn of the rum as it gracefully slid down his throat, leaving a comforting sensation in its wake. A contented smile spread across his lips, radiating warmth and happiness as his thoughts meandered back towards thoughts of Katrina. The mere mention of her name conjured a vivid rush of passionate emotions within him; a heady blend of desire, deep affection, and the tantalizing thrill of the unknown that she so effortlessly ignited within his heart. As he closed his eyes for just a moment, Jarvis could practically envision her captivating presence surrounding him like an enchanting melody. He recalled how her eyes sparkled with mischief, as if they held secrets that only he was meant to uncover. Her lips curved into that alluring smile, an expression that had initially captured his heart and drawn him into her orbit. In this blissful reverie, time seemed to stand still; the clamour of everyday life faded into an indistinct hum in the background.

All that mattered now was this intoxicating memory of Katrina, and the way she filled every crevice of his mind with colour and life. Just thinking about her was like reliving a beautiful dream from which he never wanted to awaken. Each thought about her sparked new feelings within him; it was a reminder that love can be both exhilarating and deeply grounding all at once. In this tranquil moment with only himself and his memories, intertwined with longing for her company, Jarvis felt both whole and achingly incomplete without her by his side.

"I know that look" said McMatters.

Lorraine, McMatters and Jarvis erupted into laughter, fully aware of Jarvis's affection for the younger woman. It was clear to everyone present that he revelled in the attention and adoration she had bestowed upon him. The playful teasing, and good-natured ribbing only served to further highlight the undeniable chemistry and mutual attraction between the two of them. Their colleagues couldn't help but delight in witnessing the blossoming romance unfold before their eyes, their amusement and delight palpable in the lively atmosphere.

Lorraine's phone suddenly burst into life, the shrill ringing cutting through the silence of the room. Glancing down at the device, Lorraine's heart skipped a beat as she recognized the caller ID. It was her mum, Maxine. This was highly unusual, as Maxine rarely initiated phone calls, preferring to let Lorraine reach out first. Lorraine felt a surge of concern wash over her, instantly wondering what could be so urgent that her mother felt compelled to make an uncharacteristic call.

"Mum, is everything OK?"

"Oh yes, look, can you not come home tonight?"

"Why?"

"Demetrio is coming for a meal, and you know..."

"Mum! OK, I won't come home tonight."

"Thank you, Lorraine. I plan to woo him." said Maxine

"Way too much info, Mum."

"Bye, Lorraine."

Lorraine stared at the phone; her eyes fixed on the device as she slowly shook her head in disbelief. The news she had just received had left her reeling, a whirlwind of emotions swirling within her. She couldn't believe what she had heard, the unexpected information that had Lorraine uncertain of what she had just been told.

"What's up Lorraine?" asked McMatters.

"Mum. She has Demetrio coming for a home cooked meal and wants to woo him. I so did not want that vision implanted in my brain," said Lorraine.

McMatters and Jarvis both laughed. They both knew Demetrio very well.

"Woo is more than just a woo I can tell you." Lorraine added.

"I didn't want that in my head either," said Jarvis.

Lorraine, McMatters, and Jarvis, all found themselves caught in a wave of uncontrollable laughter at the mere thought of Lorraine's mum Maxine attempting to woo the undeniably charming Demetrio. The very notion conjured up a series of images that were both comical and endearing, sending them into fits of giggles that seemed to echo throughout the room. They could hardly contain themselves as they envisioned Maxine's clumsy and awkward advances toward the object of her affection; it was simply too hilarious and absurd for them to imagine without bursting into laughter. As they roared with mirth, tears streaming down their cheeks like rivers of joy, the vivid mental picture of Maxine's earnest, yet pitiful attempts at seduction, played out in their minds like a delightful comedy sketch.

Each time they recalled her bumbling movements, punctuated by nervous stammering and flustered expressions; it only fuelled their amusement further. In stark contrast stood Demetrio, suave, confident, and effortlessly charming, his very presence magnifying the hilarity of Maxine's predicament. The juxtaposition between her endearing awkwardness and his self-assured demeanour created an endless source of delight for Lorraine, McMatters, and Jarvis. They revelled in this comedic spectacle unfolding before them, each laugh deepening their bond as friends who shared not only in the humour, but also in a genuine affection for one another's quirks. It was moments like these, when joyful camaraderie was sparked by playful teasing, that reminded them all how wonderful it was to have such cherished memories together.

Chapter nineteen
Woo Woo

Demetrio arrived promptly at Lorraine's residence, appearing right on the dot of half past five, his presence almost a beacon of anticipation. Maxine couldn't help but wonder if he had been standing outside, perhaps a little anxious, meticulously counting down the last few minutes with bated breath, before finally finding the courage to knock softly on the door. His unwavering punctuality and palpable eagerness suggested just how profoundly this meeting with Maxine mattered to him. It was as if every single second spent in anticipation held immense significance, laden with unspoken hopes and dreams. As she observed him, a wave of curiosity washed over Maxine. What fuelled Demetrio's evident enthusiasm? She found herself reflecting on their past interactions, searching for clues that might reveal whether his feelings for her ran deeper than she had initially presumed. Was it simply excitement about seeing an old friend, or did it hint at something more profound, a connection that transcended mere friendship? The thought stirred a mixture of intrigue and warmth within her heart as she pondered the possibilities that lay ahead in their unfolding story.

"Demetrio, do come in."

"It's lovely to see you again Maxine. What a wonderfully decorated home this is," said Demetrio.
"It's all Lorraine's doing. She has an eye for mixing old with new, then adds in some of the crazy smart things that are all over the place these days."

"Oh, tell me about it. Everything is smart now, not like the old days."

Maxine eagerly ushered Demetrio into the kitchen, her steps quickened with a sense of anticipation as she hurried to inspect the progress of the meal she had been meticulously preparing. The aromas wafting from the stove and oven immediately enveloped them, tantalizing their senses and heightening the excitement that filled the air. With a keen eye and a practiced hand, Maxine moved swiftly around the bustling kitchen, checking the simmering pots and the browning dishes, ensuring every element of the culinary masterpiece she was crafting was on track to perfection. Her passion for cooking and her desire to impress Demetrio with her skills were palpable in every movement, every adjustment, and every satisfied nod of her head as she surveyed the scene before her.

"I brought you a little something." Demetrio added.

"Oh, a bottle of bubbles! You're spoiling me." Maxine gasped.

Maxine couldn't help but feel a twinge of uncertainty as she contemplated inviting Demetrio to enjoy a glass or two of wine with their meal. Given Maxine's complicated history with alcohol, this was a delicate situation that required careful consideration. Maxine's mind raced with questions how would Lorraine react to the suggestion? Would she feel comfortable them indulging, or might it stir up unpleasant memories or concerns? Maxine knew she needed to tread lightly, but her desire to share an enjoyable dining experience with Demetrio was strong. With a mix of hope and trepidation, Maxine quickly composed a text message and sent it to Lorraine, eagerly awaiting her response and praying that it would signal an opportunity to navigate this sensitive issue together.

Demetrio has brought bubbles to drink with our meal. I'm not sure if you would mind?

You have done well mum. Demetrio is a good man. I'm sure a sophisticated drink would be fine; you have done very well mum.

Maxine's excitement was palpable, as evidenced by the exuberant bubbles of laughter that escaped her lips. Her joyful giggling conveyed a sense of unbridled enthusiasm and pure delight, reflecting the infectious nature of her contagious happiness. The sheer energy and vivacity radiating from Maxine's spirited outburst created an atmosphere of infectious merriment, captivating all those around her with her infectious positivity and genuine zeal. It wasn't that drinking was strictly prohibited, but after Maxine's previous struggles with using alcohol to escape her problems, her perspective on the matter had undergone a profound transformation. In the past, Maxine would often turn to drinking as a coping mechanism, a desperate attempt to numb the pain, and avoid confronting the challenges she faced. However, that destructive pattern, which contained slurred speech, aggression, violent outbursts and often collapsing in random places, has since given way to a newfound understanding and maturity about how to drink sensibly.

Now, Maxine recognizes that drinking can serve a different purpose, one of social engagement and connection. Thanks to the guidance and lessons imparted by her daughter Lorraine, Maxine has come to appreciate the value of responsible, moderate alcohol consumption, to foster camaraderie and strengthen interpersonal bonds, rather than as a means of escapism. This shift in mindset has empowered Maxine to approach social situations with a healthier, more balanced outlook, where drinking is no longer a means to an end, but rather a tool for cultivating meaningful relationships and shared experiences.

"If you get the glasses; I'll pour," said Demetrio.

Maxine tenderly handed the glasses to Demetrio, punctuating the gesture with a soft, affectionate kiss on his lips. The intimate moment conveyed the deep love and connection shared between the two individuals, highlighting the genuine warmth and passion that characterized their relationship. Maxine's actions demonstrated a level of care, intimacy, and emotional investment that went beyond the simple transfer of the physical object, infusing the mundane task with profound meaning and sentiment.

"I will set the table in the dining room."

Maxine enthusiastically began serving the delectable meal she had prepared. For the main course, she had selected a classic pasta carbonara, the rich and creamy sauce perfectly complementing the tender salmon fillets. Maxine had dusted the fish with a generous layer of grated cheese, adding a savoury and indulgent finish to the dish.

To cap off the delightful culinary experience, Maxine had lovingly crafted a decadent chocolate cake that was not only visually stunning, but also tantalizing to the taste buds. With its rich layers and a smooth, velvety buttercream centre that practically melted in your mouth, this cake was a labour of love, embodying both her passion for baking and her desire to bring joy to those around her. Crowned with plump, fresh strawberries that glistened like jewels and adorned with a generous dollop of fluffy whipped cream, the dessert promised to be an absolute delight for the senses, an exquisite treat that would serve as a sweet and indulgent conclusion to their sumptuous feast.

As Maxine and Demetrio sat down together at the elegantly set table, they immersed themselves in each other's company, savouring not just the flavours, but also the warmth of their shared connection. The gentle clinking of champagne flutes filled the air as they toasted to shared memories and future adventures. Each sip of bubbly champagne complemented the rich decadence of the cake, creating an atmosphere brimming with laughter and heartfelt conversation. In this moment, surrounded by delicious food and each other's presence, it felt as if time stood still. A beautiful reminder of life's simple yet profound pleasures.

Chapter Twenty

Detective Winters

Detective Winters was puzzled by the information she had received about a large group of men turning up near a known drug dealer's location. This discovery raised several concerns and questions in her mind. The presence of a sizable gathering near a suspected narcotics trafficker, was an unusual occurrence that warranted further investigation. Detective Winters knew she needed to delve deeper to uncover the underlying reasons, and potential implications behind this suspicious activity. Without more context or details, the situation remained perplexing, and she felt compelled to explore the matter further to determine if any illicit or nefarious actions were taking place. Detective Winters, concerned about the suspicious group of men, deployed a team of undercover officers to conduct surveillance in the area. The plan was for the officers to blend in with the public and observe the group's activities more closely. However, on each attempt to get nearer to the group, the officers were met with resistance and were forced to retreat or move away from the location. This suggests that the group was highly cautious and vigilant, making it challenging for the police to gather more information or make any progress in their investigation.

The group's ability to detect and deter the undercover officers' efforts highlighted their heightened awareness and the need for the police to devise a more strategic approach to monitor them. Based on the feedback provided, it appears the situation raises more questions than answers, as the information seems to indicate that the men are shielding a known drug dealer. But from what? Or who?

This is a concerning development that warrants further scrutiny, as protecting individuals engaged in illegal and harmful activities, such as drug dealing, can enable the continuation of such behaviour and undermine efforts to maintain public safety and the rule of the Law. Why was the extra security needed? Who provided the extra security? Who was after the drug dealer? Is this a turf war? Who were all the parties involved? Detective Winters worked overtime, trying to find answers to the questions, but each time she hit a brick wall.

Blythe

Blythe's primary concern was not the potential threats, intimidation, or violence that he might face, but rather the uncertainty surrounding the identity and nature of the Slaters. The lack of information about this group left him feeling anxious and unsettled, as he was unsure of what to expect or how to prepare for any potential interactions with them. This sense of the unknown, rather than specific fears of harm, was the primary driver of Blythe's worries in this situation. Blythe felt a sense of temporary relief and security now, given the additional security measures and personnel that were now assisting with the sale of the stock from the shipment that had been delivered successfully.

However, this feeling of safety was likely fragile and fleeting, as the underlying circumstances that necessitated the heightened security presence were still a cause for concern. Blythe may have been apprehensive about the long-term stability and sustainability of the situation, knowing that the challenges that had led to the need for these extra precautions had not yet been fully resolved.

Blythe was deeply appreciative of the support and assistance provided by Lorraine and Jarvis, as the

Blythes had found themselves in a rather precarious situation following an incident that had occurred at the club. The help and understanding offered by these trusted companions were invaluable, as the Blythes grappled with the aftermath and implications of their actions.

Without the steadfast backing of Lorraine and Jarvis, Blythe may have found the situation much more daunting and difficult to navigate. Blythe was growing increasingly anxious and concerned about the situation surrounding the Slaters. He desperately hoped that someone would be able to quickly identify and uncover the identity of the Slaters, as the uncertainty and lack of information was weighing heavily on his mind.

Blythe felt an urgent need to understand who these Slaters were and what their involvement or connection might be, as the suspense and ambiguity of the circumstances was causing him significant worry and distress. He fervently wished that the truth would come to light soon, as the lingering questions and lack of clarity were taking an emotional toll.

Chapter Twenty-One

Progress

McMatters' was worried that the rapid succession of recent events and developments might be too overwhelming and challenging for Lorraine to manage effectively. The sheer volume and pace of changes occurring in such a short time span risked becoming too much for Lorraine to handle comfortably. McMatters' was concerned that Lorraine might struggle to process and adapt to all the new circumstances, potentially leading to increased stress or difficulty coping. There was a sense that the cumulative impact of the recent events could prove too taxing and burdensome for Lorraine. She might need additional time to process events. McMatters' decided to get Jarvis's candid perspective on whether he believes Lorraine will be able to handle or cope with the challenges and uncertainties that lie ahead. By seeking Jarvis's direct and honest assessment of the situation, McMatters hoped to gain an insight into Jarvis's assessment of Lorraine's ability to navigate the difficulties that are likely to emerge soon.

"Jarvis, can we talk about something that is concerning me?" said McMatters.

"Fire away. I'm all ears."

"How do you think Lorraine has handled everything so far? She's still new to all this."

"She's done quite well, really. It's odd, but she's taken to it like a duck to water. Almost like something in her past that maybe she's had to do."

"Do you think she has what it takes to do what's needed?"

"I asked her the same thing, as I wanted to know if she thought she could go all the way. She wasn't sure about it, because she hadn't been in the situation before, but I do know something has changed in her since she was attacked."

"I had seen the change in her. She's more confident, but I haven't known her long enough to know if she has always had this within her."

"I understand where you're coming from. I told her if we're in a situation and she isn't comfortable doing what's needed, she's to give me the nod and I'll take over."

"Good plan. Thanks for looking out for her Jarvis."
"Don't mention it. All is good."

McMatters felt a sense of relief knowing that Jarvis was keeping an eye on Lorraine and would be there to lend a hand if she needed it. Lorraine was still in the process of getting the hang of things, and it was reassuring to have someone experienced like Jarvis looking out for her, and willing to step in and provide guidance or assistance if she requested it. Having that safety net in place helped put McMatters' mind at ease, as they knew Lorraine would have the support she needed while she continued to develop her skills and knowledge.

Lorraine will be keeping the bodyguards assigned to her on a permanent basis, as he felt it was necessary for her own sense of security and well-being. The presence of the security personnel provided Lorraine with a greater feeling of safety and reassurance, which he deemed essential given the circumstances. He recognized the importance of her having the bodyguards continue their protective duties indefinitely, as it contributed to his overall peace of mind as well.

Lorraine

Lorraine sauntered up to the club's entrance after her driver dropped her off half hour before the doors were set to open for the evening, exuding confidence in her stylish ensemble. The sleek black suit she had donned was accented with a vibrant purple trim, perfectly complemented by the eye-catching purple shoes adorning her feet. Lorraine couldn't help but feel a sense of pride and swagger as she took in her reflection, knowing she was absolutely crushing the dress code, and was sure to turn heads once the night got underway. Lorraine strutted into the office, planting a vibrant purple lipstick laden smooch directly on the unsuspecting lips of McMatters. Fully embracing the colour scheme for the evening, she then gracefully settled into her trusty, amethyst hued office chair. Feeling a deep sense of preparedness, Lorraine poured herself a refreshing "Purple Rain" cocktail from the nearby decanter, taking a restorative sip as she steeled herself for the festivities ahead. The evening commenced with a vibrant and lively atmosphere as the packed nightclub pulsed with energy. The music, a familiar and beloved soundtrack, reverberated through the space, setting the mood for a thrilling night of revelry. The air crackled with an electric buzz, as patrons eagerly anticipated the festivities that lay ahead, ready to lose themselves in the infectious rhythm and excitement of the evening's revelries, everyone was enjoying themselves. At precisely eleven in the evening, Jarvis's phone suddenly sprang to life, the shrill ring piercing the tranquil silence of the dimly lit office. This unexpected call would soon set in motion a chain of events, that would prove to be far more captivating and entertaining than the monotony of Jarvis's typical workday. With a mix of trepidation and curiosity, Jarvis tentatively answers the phone, bracing himself for whatever peculiar twist of fate is about to unfold before him.

"Hi Bennett, how are you doing?" said Jarvis.

"Not bad Jarvis, but you're going to like the information one of my lads just found out" replied Bennett.

"I'm all ears." Jarvis sits forward attentively.

"It's the Slaters. I've not found them yet, but we know where their stash house is."

"Oooh, I'm liking this indeed. Grab three men from each family. We are on our way. Text me the location?"

"Will do. This little action sounds like fun."

Left at the barn on lakeside way, second right, last outbuilding.

"Got it. See you there," said Jarvis.

Jarvis was filled with a bubbling sense of excitement as he eagerly anticipated his visit to the clandestine stash house. With a sparkle in his eye, he rubbed his hands together, each motion reflecting the glee that danced within him. The thrill of potential payback loomed large in his mind, igniting a longing for the kind of exhilarating experiences that can only be found on the edge of this sort of mischief. The thought of engaging in some good old-fashioned excitement sent a delightful shiver down his spine, an electrifying promise of adventure waiting just around the corner. As he plotted his next move, Jarvis felt like a kid on the brink of an escapade, grinning from ear to ear as wild ideas raced through his head. He envisioned moments filled with adrenaline and laughter, where every heartbeat echoed with anticipation. In this world teetering between risk and reward, Jarvis couldn't help but feel drawn to the allure of rebellion, a magnetic pull that promised not only thrills, but also a temporary escape from the humdrum reality of daily life.

"Okay Lorraine, we are up. Time for some fun" said Jarvis smiling.
"I can't wait to find out what," said Lorraine.

"We have found the Slaters' stash house."

"Nice job Jarvis. Let's go and show them how it's done" said McMatters.

Lorraine and Jarvis made a stealthy exit from the club through the rear entrance, while McMatters remained inside. It was crucial that McMatters only made an appearance when necessary to maintain a facade of presence. This strategic move would ensure McMatters' grand reveal would be perfectly timed, coinciding with the moment they finally tracked down the elusive Slaters.

Chapter Twenty-Two
Maxine

Maxine and Demetrio thoroughly enjoyed a delightful dining experience together. They savoured a sumptuous meal in the cosy, welcoming ambiance of Lorraine's dining room, relishing each flavourful bite. As the sun began to dip below the horizon, painting the sky in vibrant hues, the couple moved outside to continue their celebration. There, they indulged in a slice of rich, decadent cake and sipped on refreshing champagne, toasting to the beauty of the sunset and the joy of each other's company. It was a truly magical evening filled with laughter, warmth, and the simple pleasures of good food, good drinks, and good company.

"Maxine, let's put on some music and dance while the sunset fades." said Demetrio

"Oh, what a wonderful idea." Maxine said thinking she could get used to this.

Maxine couldn't help but feel a sense of joyful wonder as she asked the smart system to play some romantic music for her to dance to. To her pleasant surprise, the system responded seamlessly, effortlessly curating a selection of soothing, melodic tunes that filled the room. Maxine marvelled at the system's intuitive understanding of her request, impressed by its ability to provide the perfect ambiance for her impromptu dance. With a smile on her face, she gracefully moved to the rhythm, lost in the moment and marvelling at the sheer convenience and responsiveness of the smart technology at her fingertips. The experience still amazed Maxine, reminding her of the profound ways in which intelligent systems can enhance everyday life, and foster moments of pure delight. Maxine and Demetrio danced with unbridled joy, their bodies moving in perfect synchronicity as they lost themselves in the rhythm of the music.

Time seemed to stand still as they revelled in the sheer delight of being in each other's embrace, their steps light and graceful, every twirl and spin a testament to the deep connection that they shared. The dance floor became their own private sanctuary, where they could escape the world and simply bask in the euphoric bliss of the moment, their hearts beating as one.

As the evening came to an end, Maxine yearned for more. But she was uncertain if Demetrio shared the same sentiment. Mustering up the courage, Maxine gently leaned in and placed a tender kiss upon Demetrio's lips. To Maxine's delighted surprise, Demetrio reciprocated the affectionate gesture, filling Maxine's heart with unbridled joy and elation. In that moment, Maxine's apprehension melted away, replaced by a sense of profound happiness and connection as the two shared a magical, intimate encounter. Maxine took Demetrio's hand and led him upstairs

"Are you sure Maxine? I don't want to rush you."

Maxine leaned in with a joyful glow, planting a passionate kiss upon his eager lips. Filled with excitement, she reached out and tenderly grasped his hand, intertwining their fingers as they continued their ascent. Ascending the stairs together, their hearts racing with anticipation of what awaited them upstairs.

Chapter Twenty-Three
Karen

Karen was in an exhilarated, almost euphoric state, filled with a palpable eagerness to engage in a few thrilling games. Emboldened by her spirited disposition, Karen was utterly resolute and would not accept any refusal. She was determined to get her way. In her mind, the captivating Steve belonged solely to her, and that other woman, the alluring Lorraine, would most certainly not be allowed to stake any claim on him. Karen's possessiveness and intensity bordered on the obsessive, as she sought to firmly cement her dominance over the situation. Karen dressed herself for the special event with great care and intention, selecting a revealing crop top and a daringly short mini skirt. This provocative ensemble was purposefully designed to allow for easy and convenient access, prioritizing function over form. Completing the look, Karen donned a pair of towering high heeled shoes, creating a striking visual contrast despite the apparent lack of coordination between the disparate elements of her outfit. Exuding an air of unbridled confidence, Karen paid no mind to the potential incongruity of her ensemble, fully embracing her own unique sense of style and personal expression on this momentous occasion.

Karen carelessly swept her dishevelled, unkempt hair up into a messy, haphazard pony. This was a clear indication that it had not been properly tended to or groomed for an extended period, likely weeks since it had last seen the cleansing touch of a brush or the rejuvenating effect of a thorough washing. The disorderly state of her hair was a striking visual representation of the apparent neglect and disarray, encompassing her personal appearance and self-care routine and then, with an almost ethereal grace, she delicately applied a fresh layer of makeup over the remnants of her previous night's cosmetic artistry. The process was a mesmerizing display of skill and precision. She expertly blended the new pigments into the existing facial canvas, creating a seamless, radiant transformation. Onlookers were shocked by her mastery of the craft, which now made her look like a clown.

The thoughts of Steve, her beloved Steve, consumed Karen's mind, swirling endlessly like a stormy sea. He was the beacon of light in her life, and she found herself utterly captivated by the image of him, his warm smile, the way his laughter danced in the air like music that only she could hear, and how her heart overflowed with adoration for every little thing he did. Yet this blissful reverie was suddenly shattered by the intrusive presence of another, a wretched individual who had dared to come between them: Lorraine.

A burning rage ignited within Karen, a righteous fury that demanded retribution for what felt like an unprovoked assault on her very happiness. In her mind's eye, she could vividly envision herself unleashing the full force of her wrath upon this vile usurper, giving them both barrels, as it were, ensuring they faced not just consequences, but a reckoning for their transgressions against love and loyalty. Karen was left utterly humiliated and devastated by Lorraine's cruel and demeaning actions at the club that night. The memory loomed large: Lorraine's callous behaviour as she dragged Karen out by her hair, like some wild animal, an act so barbaric it transcended mere cruelty, it felt truly horrific and dehumanizing. The sheer brutality displayed by Lorraine revealed an unsettling lack of compassion, that was not only appalling, but also deeply unsettling to witness. Rest assured; Lorraine will undoubtedly face repercussions for her heinous actions; justice will find its way to her doorstep. She will be made to suffer for what she has done and may even beg for mercy when confronted with the fallout from her cruelty. Of that, there is no doubt in Karen's mind. The mere thought of Lorraine finally receiving the retribution that she so richly deserves, is a prospect both chilling and awe-inspiring. It fills one with a sense of grim satisfaction, as if balance might finally be restored in a world where love should reign supreme over hatred.

Chapter Twenty-Four
The Stash House

Lorraine and Jarvis cautiously approached the secluded stash house, keeping a low profile. The Bennetts and the Santos had already arrived and had strategically parked their vehicles out of sight. Closely following Jarvis and Lorraine from the main road was the new family, the Blythe's, accompanied by a car full of Jarvis's men. This coordinated arrival ensured their presence at the stash house remained concealed from any potential onlookers, or adversaries. Jarvis quickly assembled the team, gathering them into a tight huddle so that they could speak in hushed, discreet tones. The close-knit formation allowed the group to communicate quietly and strategically, ensuring their discussion remained private and out of earshot of any unwanted observers. Jarvis took the lead, motioning for the others to draw in closer as he prepared to outline the next steps in their important mission.

"Okay, we need to all surround the house and form a cordon, we have enough here to achieve it. Then we all move in slowly and silently; the element of surprise will achieve a better outcome. Once we are tucked up next to the house, two men front and back to stay outside, everyone else goes in as quickly as possible .... We take the lot!" Said Jarvis.

"Will do." They all agreed.

"Once empty, we all meet back at Blythe's," said Lorraine.
The huddle broke, and they all went to take their positions, Jarvis handed Lorraine a Glock, "use two hands, she's got a kick." Lorraine nodded. "Don't move from my side." Lorraine nodded.

"We watching boss" said Lorraine's body guards.

The stash house was strategically nestled in the heart of an unkempt, overgrown field, where tall, scraggy blades of grass swayed gently in the breeze. This dishevelled yet natural camouflage enveloped the location, making it an ideal hideaway for concealing the illicit operation from any prying eyes that might wander too close. Jarvis, fully aware of the gravity of their situation, cautiously raised his hand and brought it down in a decisive motion, a silent signal to his companions that they needed to proceed with utmost care. As they all began to move forward slowly and steadily towards the secluded house, a palpable tension hung in the air. Each member of the group understood all too well that discretion and vigilance were paramount. As they approached this clandestine destination shrouded in mystery. The atmosphere was thick with uncertainty; no one could say with certainty whether anyone was inside that seemingly abandoned structure, or how heavily armed those insides might be.

The weight of their mission pressed upon them like a heavy fog, amplifying their senses as they navigated through the tall grass. Each rustle and whisper became amplified, heightening their awareness to both potential threats, and hidden dangers lurking within that isolated place. However, everyone was aware of the unspoken rules that still governed, Jarvis rules, the established code of the proverbial "good old days." The understanding was clear: no man could bring harm to a woman or could lay a hand on a child. If a woman required some form of disciplinary action, it could only be administered by another woman.

As Jarvis approached the weathered walls of the house, a sense of urgency filled the air. He grasped the cold handle, his heart racing with anticipation, only to be met with disappointment when he discovered that the door was firmly locked. An unsettling stillness enveloped him for a moment, but he shook off any lingering doubt and stepped back to communicate with the rest of his team. With unwavering resolve, he relayed what he had encountered; there was no time to waste. In a perfect synchronization that spoke to their training and camaraderie, the leader of the Bennett group took charge. Each member fell silent as they prepared for action, an unspoken bond connecting them in this tense moment. On Jarvis's count of three, they launched themselves forward with determination; powerful kicks collided forcefully against the doors. The sound echoed like thunder in their ears as both doors burst open simultaneously, revealing what lay beyond. Without hesitation or fear, they surged into the dimly lit interior of the house. Instinctively dropping low to maintain a defensive posture, they braced themselves for whatever might lurk inside, each aware that their safety depended on their unity and quick thinking in this unpredictable situation. The atmosphere was thick with tension, but also infused with a shared sense of purpose; together they would face whatever challenges awaited them within those walls.

Chapter Twenty-Five

Rosy Glow

Maxine's face was beaming with pure joy, a radiant smile stretching from one ear to the other. She had never imagined that her life could feel this way, overflowing with happiness and contentment. Meeting Demetrio had been a life-changing experience for Maxine, as he treated her with the utmost care and respect, making her feel like a true princess. For the first time, Maxine fully understood what it meant to be deeply happy, and at peace within a loving relationship. The connection she shared with Demetrio had exceeded all her previous expectations, filling her heart with a profound sense of fulfilment that she had never experienced before.

Why had she never stumbled upon this hidden gem before? Yet, in a strange way, she was grateful that she hadn't. For if she had, then Maxine may have never crossed paths with the captivating Demetrio. It's remarkable how the universe operates in such mysterious, and often serendipitous ways, guiding us towards the people and experiences that are meant to be part of our lives. This chance encounter has unfolded in the most curious and delightful manner, leaving her in awe of the invisible forces that orchestrate the unfolding of our lives. The way things have worked out is truly humorous and profound, a testament to the unpredictable nature of life's journey. Maxine was curled up in Demetrio's embrace, basking in the warm afterglow of their lovemaking. This was the first time they had shared such an intimate moment since the start of their blossoming relationship, and Maxine's heart was overflowing with a profound sense of joy and fulfilment. While Demetrio had drifted off to sleep not long after their passionate encounter, Maxine remained wide awake, savouring every exquisite second of the comfort and security, that now enveloped her like a warm blanket on a cold winter night. She relished the sensation of Demetrio's strong, protective arms wrapped around her, an embrace that felt both safe and reassuring, as if he were her personal fortress against the world. The deep connection they had forged in that fleeting moment, was more than just physical; it was an intertwining of their souls that transcended words, echoing through the silence of the night. Maxine couldn't help but reflect on how rare such moments were, how they had carved out a space in time where only they existed, free from outside distractions or worries. She was determined to commit this experience to memory, allowing herself to bask in the glow of their profound emotional and physical intimacy. Each heartbeat seemed to resonate with love and tenderness, reinforcing her resolve to hold onto this precious memory long after the night faded into dawn. As time passed and the gentle rhythm of Demetrio's breathing lulled her further into contentment, it wasn't too long before Maxine herself succumbed to sleep. A serene smile lingered on her face, a testament to the joy she felt in that moment as she drifted off into dreams filled with echoes of laughter and the love shared between them. In those quiet hours, wrapped in his embrace, she felt truly at peace.

Chapter Twenty-Six
The Club

Karen found herself in a familiar predicament as she arrived at the club. With just enough funds to cover the entrance fee and procure a single drink, she felt a growing sense of frustration and desperation. This had become an all-too-common occurrence in her life lately, as she was forced to compromise her dignity and self-respect, merely to secure the meagre resources needed for necessities. Initially, it had been a struggle to afford food, but as time went on, the challenges only compounded. Keeping warm and dry had become an additional burden, compelling her to seek out temporary shelter. Yet even that proved difficult, given the soaring costs of rent these days.

Karen was trapped in a vicious cycle, having to repeatedly "sell herself out," just to scrape by; a situation that was weighing heavily on her sense of self-worth and autonomy. Karen was fully aware that her Steve, had substantial financial resources at his disposal. She was confident that with his ample wealth, he would be able to comfortably provide for her and ensure she would never have to struggle or scrimp to get by. All Karen needed to do was find a way to deal with the problematic presence of that woman, the "bitch" who she perceived as a threat to her financial security, and her relationship with Steve. Karen was determined to find a solution that would allow her to maintain her comfortable lifestyle and secure Steve's continued support, even if it meant confronting, or removing the perceived obstacle standing in her way. Karen confidently strode up to the bar, intent on ordering a refreshing drink. As she approached, she couldn't help but notice the barman's gaze lingering on her in a way that made her feel dirty, as if she were merely an obstacle he had to navigate, rather than a valued customer. Feeling disrespected and determined to address this unprofessional behaviour, Karen decided she would get Steve to fire him. "That will teach him!" she thought. As Karen surveyed the club's interior, it was not her first time in the club, but the last time she had gone straight upstairs as the club wasn't open at the time.

However, she couldn't help but notice the remarkable transformation that had taken place. The decor and furnishings exuded an air of sophistication and quality, leaving no doubt that Steve had invested considerable effort and resources into elevating the establishment. The attention to detail and the overall aesthetic, suggested that he had not merely settled for a basic or inexpensive approach, but had instead meticulously curated an environment that conveyed a sense of luxury and refinement.

Karen's keen observation of the club's impressive surroundings, served as a heartfelt testament to Steve's successful endeavours, and his remarkable ability to create a truly captivating atmosphere that drew people in from all walks of life. The nightclub, alive with energy and excitement, was bustling with activity, particularly around the crowded bar area, where laughter and music intermingled in a joyful symphony. However, amidst the vibrant chaos, Karen began to feel overwhelmed by the sheer volume of the sights and sounds surrounding her. To regain her composure, she decided to move away from the pulsating bar scene and take a step back to survey her surroundings more thoughtfully.

As she paused for a moment, taking in the lively crowd dancing under shimmering lights and enjoying their drinks, something caught her attention: several patrons nearby seemed to be holding their noses with expressions of discomfort on their faces. This unexpected reaction sent a jolt of concern through Karen; it was clear that an unpleasant odour had permeated the air. In that instant, Karen's heart sank as she began to wonder if perhaps, she had forgotten one crucial element of her evening routine, applying deodorant before leaving home. The thought loomed over her like an unwelcome shadow, prompting feelings of embarrassment mixed with anxiety. Determined not to let this potential faux pas ruin her night, or affect those around her, she quickly made her way toward the restrooms in search of relief, a discreet moment where she could address this nagging concern and ensure that she could fully enjoy herself among friends without any lingering worries clouding her mind.

Chapter Twenty-Seven
The Stash House

As the chaotic scene unfolded, everyone stormed the illicit drug stash house simultaneously, with a sense of urgency and unwavering determination. Both the front and back entrances were swiftly and forcefully breached, creating a cacophony of shattering glass and splintering wood, that reverberated through the dimly lit corridors. This unsettling symphony served as a harbinger of the imminent demise of a guarded operation, that was shrouded in secrecy and desperation. The hapless occupants, taken completely off guard by this sudden and overwhelming raid, found themselves frozen in shock, as they watched helplessly from their hiding spots. Their faces reflecting a mix of fear and disbelief, as they witnessed their criminal enterprise unravelling before their very eyes in a dramatic display of authority and control. Once considered an impregnable fortress that seemed invulnerable to outside threats, this haven for illicit activities had been thoroughly dismantled with precision from both sides.

In that moment, it was not just about the loss of possessions or freedom; it was also about shattered dreams and lives disrupted by choices made under duress. Everyone inside had their own story, a complex tapestry woven from challenging circumstances that led them down this perilous path. The raid marked not only an end to their operations, but also served as a stark reminder of the harsh realities faced by those entangled in such dangerous lifestyles. As the walls crumbled around them, so too did the fragile illusions they had built to justify their actions.

Once the entryway was secured, Lorraine and Jarvis made their grand entrance, striding in from opposite directions with a palpable air of confidence. The longer they took to reach the centre of the room, the more the three Slaters visibly squirmed, their eyes betraying a growing sense of dread and unease. As the two imposing figures converged, Jarvis couldn't resist a subtle nod towards the leader of the Bennetts, silently communicating a message of dominance and control. The Stash house presented an unsettling sight, embodying a state of disrepair that spoke volumes about its neglect. The air was heavy with a sense of desolation, as the once sturdy structure now succumbed to the ravages of time and weather. Its walls bore the scars of deterioration, with broken wooden planks jutting out at odd angles, and gaping holes where it seemed they had been violently smashed in by some unseen force. In several corners, patches of mould crept along the surfaces, thriving in the dampness that clung to the air like a shroud. Adding to this eerie tableau, weeds defiantly sprouted from cracks in the floorboards, and crevices in the walls, claiming their space within this forsaken abode. It was as if nature itself was reclaiming territory from a place long abandoned by human care and attention.

"Tie them up," said Jarvis.

Jarvis regarded Lorraine with a bemused expression, his eyes twinkling with both amusement and respect, as he grandly swept his arm in a sweeping gesture that wordlessly invited her to take charge of the unfolding situation.

Lorraine stood tall and resolute, embodying the very essence of cool confidence. Without missing a beat, she deftly tucked the gun into her waistband, a move that spoke volumes about her composure, and sauntered over to the Bennetts' impressive display of blades, each one gleaming under the soft light like a promise waiting to be fulfilled. Her discerning gaze roamed over the array of weaponry before homing in on a sleek, short-bladed arcing knife, that seemed to call out to her with an almost magnetic allure.

The craftsmanship was exquisite, and its design hinted at both elegance and lethal efficiency. With an air of quiet determination, she silently extended her hand towards it; her intent was as clear as day, this was no mere idle interest; she meant to wield this blade. In response to Lorraine's bold move, the leader of the Bennetts exchanged a knowing glance with Jarvis, an unspoken understanding passing between them that acknowledged her capability and resolve. Jarvis nodded affirmatively, signalling that he trusted Lorraine completely in this moment where stakes were high. Without so much as a moment's hesitation or reluctance, the blade was handed over to Lorraine, a gesture imbued not just with acceptance, but also with an acknowledgment of her strength and potential, as they all faced what lay ahead together.

The air was thick with an unspoken understanding that these were not individuals to be trifled with. The tension in the room was palpable, a silent acknowledgment of the power dynamics at play. Lorraine's hush-hush performance, meticulously orchestrated and executed with precision, truly sent shockwaves reverberating through the Slaters' stash house. What began as an ordinary evening swiftly transformed into a gripping experience, that would be etched indelibly into their memories, like a vivid painting upon the canvas of their lives. As the three men lay there, bound and gagged on the cold floor, each moment felt heavy with tension and anticipation, creating an almost suffocating atmosphere that clung to them like fog.

Suddenly, in this high-stakes environment rife with fear and uncertainty, one of them found himself grappling with an unexpected predicament that highlighted his vulnerability in stark contrast to their earlier bravado. Utterly unable to maintain control over his overactive bladder, a situation both humiliating and distressing, he became a victim of his own body's betrayal at perhaps the worst possible moment. It had become all too regular for members of this criminal underworld to encounter confrontations involving Jarvis or other notorious figures like the Bennetts or Santos. They were known for instilling fear and commanding respect through sheer force of personality alone. But now, amidst this tense standoff engineered by Lorraine's cunning tactics, she had succeeded not just in asserting power, but also in making someone wet their pants, a profound illustration of how fear can strip away dignity in an instant.

It was a reminder of our humanity, even within such dark circumstances, a potent mix of shame and vulnerability enveloping them all as they faced the consequences of their choices under Lorraine's unwavering gaze, the funny side of this was Lorraine hadn't even got started. The air was charged with a peculiar mix of horror and amusement, as the unsuspecting audience bore witness to this unfolding drama. Their laughter, muffled and restrained, echoed softly in the dimly lit room, an almost surreal soundtrack that contrasted sharply with the gravity of the situation at hand. The absurdity of it all painted a vivid scene; it was as if life had taken a sharp turn into dark comedy, leaving everyone present caught between sympathy for the man's plight, and amusement at the unexpected turn events had taken.
Jarvis puffed out his chest, beaming with pride as he recounted Lorraine's impressive accomplishments.

She had mastered the art of control, expertly directing her forces with an iron fist, all without laying a single finger on the enemy. It was a true testament to her strategic brilliance and tactical prowess. Jarvis couldn't help but feel a twinge of envy, wishing he possessed

Lorraine's uncanny ability to vanquish her foes without even ruffling a hair on their heads. She will be a great leader one day he thought, watching her in motion. Lorraine sauntered over to the three captives bound on the floor, a mischievous glint in her eye.

"Get these idiots up on their feet," she ordered, her voice dripping with saccharine sweetness.

In an instant, several henchmen sprang into action, roughly hauling the hapless prisoners into a standing position. Lorraine twirled the blade in her hand, the steel flashing wickedly as she drank in the terror etched across the captives' faces.

"Empty this place of all products," Lorraine commanded, her voice dripping with authority.

One of the captured individuals, quivering in fear, couldn't hold back the tears streaming down his face. Jarvis, on the other hand, fought the overwhelming urge to burst out laughing at the spectacle unfolding before him. As Jarvis scanned the room, he noticed the rapt attention of everyone present. They were all eagerly anticipating the show, wondering just how much torture Lorraine would inflict.

Having witnessed Jarvis in action, they knew first-hand the extent of his capabilities. But now, they were faced with a woman in the driver's seat. Many had not seen what Lorraine could do, and only the leaders of each family had witnessed that Lorraine had a gift for words, that could cut the air with a knife, and some couldn't help but feel a sense of unease. After all, who knew what a woman in control was capable of? Lorraine strode towards the three captives with a mischievous glint in her eye.

"Strip them bare!" she commanded, her voice dripping with a newfound confidence.

Jarvis could sense that even though Lorraine was making it up as she went along, she was starting to find her groove. This power-hungry persona was clearly resonating with her, and she was revelling in the thrill of it all. Perhaps, Jarvis mused nervously, he had inadvertently unleashed a formidable force, a veritable monster of his own creation. Either that, or it was always there, just waiting to be released.

Lorraine strolled around the trio of unclothed men, twirling the blade with an effortless finesse that seemed almost otherworldly. Jarvis, utterly bewildered by this unexpected exhibition, had no inkling that Lorraine possessed such formidable blade-handling skills; it was indeed a surprising and astonishing development. No one had witnessed the precise moment when her prowess transformed into something terrifyingly lethal, but in a heartbeat, all three men bore fresh gashes across their chests, deep and crimson lines that spoke volumes of Lorraine's chilling talent.

As she continued her ominous circling, the rhythmic motion of her blade created an eerie dance that mesmerized her onlookers. The hapless captives were reduced to blubbering wrecks. Their faces pale with shock and fear, as crimson rivulets traced the contours of their wounds, cascading down their bodies, like grotesque ribbons of life spilling forth from their injuries. It was a startling display, a visceral tableau vivant that left spectators slack-jawed and grappling with the harrowing realization of Lorraine's deadly capabilities.

Before anyone could fully comprehend what had transpired, the three individuals had sustained more than a dozen gruesome slashes; yet not one among the audience could assert they had seen the blade contact any flesh. Instead, it was as if Lorraine wielded not just a weapon, but an artist's brush, transforming human skin into a veritable canvas splashed with vivid crimson, an abstract display that now marred the floor beneath them in grim splendour.

The scene resembled that of a deranged artist who had gone on a rampage; each stroke reckless yet calculated in its execution, resulting in what could only be described as a macabre masterpiece amidst the carnage. In this chaotic moment filled with tension and horror, Lorraine cast a glance over at Jarvis. To her surprise, and perhaps amusement, he wore a self-satisfied grin on his face, a contrast to the grim spectacle unfolding around them. His amused expression seemed to please Lorraine immensely; she couldn't help but crack a small smile herself in response to Jarvis' apparent delight, as if his cheerful demeanour was somehow contagious amid such darkness. The two shared an intimate moment of levity amidst the chaos, their eyes met for just an instant, a subtle yet playful exchange passing silently between them without words spoken aloud. Yet even amidst this unexpected camaraderie laced with humour, Lorraine knew she must return her attention to the task at hand. The swirling energy around her demanded it. But for just those fleeting moments, connected by shared glances and smiles amidst turmoil, it felt like an oasis within the storm surrounding them.

"Where is your boss?"

"I will never tell!" defiantly proclaimed one of the three suspects.

Lorraine, determined to extract the information, swiftly moved in and, with a swift slash of her blade, severed the man's, ahem, "tiny man piece."

The resulting agonizing screams were enough to make one's ears bleed. Unfazed, Lorraine then delivered the coup de grace, slashing the man's throat in a clean swift movement. He crumpled to the floor, his life force rapidly ebbing away.

"One down, two to go," Lorraine repeated, her tone dripping with sarcasm as she eyed the remaining perpetrators. "Now, tell me, where might your illustrious leader be hiding?"

One of the thugs, his bravado clearly shaken, let out a defiant cry. "Screw you, you're an old hag!" he spat, his words laced with venom.

Lorraine simply quirked an eyebrow, an amused smirk playing on her lips. "Oh, dear, it appears we have a bit of a potty mouth on our hands." Without further ado, she strode over to the miscreant, stabbing him repeatedly until the last part of life drained from his body. "Tsk, tsk, such a shame. I do hope you've learned your lesson about respecting your elders."

Jarvis was utterly gobsmacked! He stopped counting after the seventh time Lorraine stabbed the body. Jarvis gazed upon Lorraine, he nearly choked on his own tongue at the sheer skill of words: of what she had just said, and then done. Lorraine's once pristine appearance in her new suit had been transformed into a veritable Jackson Pollock painting, with splotches and spatters of crimson covering her skin, her suit, hair, face and quite frankly, most of the entire team and their crew. Jarvis couldn't help but wonder, "How in the ever-loving name of Queen Elizabeth did this happen?" Jarvis didn't know Lorraine had it in her. He was shocked, as he surveyed the carnage that had unfolded before his very eyes. And there he stood, the lone survivor of the Slater Stash house crew, his trousers soaked in a testament to his sheer terror.

"Where is your boss?" Lorraine said in a demanding tone, that screamed please do give me a reason to inflict all the pain you could dream of.

The man's body trembled uncontrollably, each convulsion a testament to his overwhelming fear, as the desperate words spilled forth from his quivering lips. "Please, don't kill me! I'll tell you everything!" he implored, his voice breaking with a mixture of terror and desperation.

In a heart-wrenching display of vulnerability, he fell to his knees, the dust and dirt of the ground clinging to him like the weight of impending doom. Tears streamed down his face, glistening in the faint light as they traced paths through the grime, each droplet a silent witness to his anguish and surrender. In that moment, he was not just a man pleading for his life; he was a soul laid bare, grappling with the rawness of fear and remorse, hoping against hope that compassion might still find its way into this dire situation.

Lorraine, unfazed by the man's hysterics, simply turned to Jarvis and nodded. "He's all yours," then walked out of the house, leaving the poor, wet-panted fellow to his own devices.

 It was a scene straight out of a bad action movie, complete with a hapless, cowardly henchman and a cold, calculated villain making a dramatic exit.

"Santos get the info we need, everything you can!" said Jarvis.

Jarvis

Jarvis hurried to the back of the car, his heart racing with a mixture of concern and determination as he frantically rummaged through the boot in search of some bags for poor Lorraine. She was in a truly dire state, absolutely drenched in what could only be described as an alarming amount of blood. Understanding the gravity of the situation, Jarvis knew he had to act swiftly to provide Lorraine with a suitable seat cover. He couldn't bear the thought of her leaving behind a grisly crime scene, a trail of crimson staining every inch of the pristine upholstery in his precious forty-five-thousand-pound car. With urgency fuelling his actions, he tossed aside spare tires and a jumble of cables, that cluttered the space around him, desperate to find something that would offer her at least a semblance of comfort amidst such chaos. At long last, after what felt like an eternity searching through items that seemed utterly irrelevant now, his hands landed upon a stack of paper grocery bags tucked away at the far corner, a serendipitous discovery that might serve as just the makeshift throne Lorraine needed, in her bloodied yet unbowed condition. With careful precision and compassion for his friend's plight, Jarvis quickly gathered them up. It was a small gesture, but one filled with empathy and urgency—an attempt to ease not just her physical discomfort, but also preserve some of her dignity during this harrowing moment.

"Steve!" Jarvis phoned him urgently.

"What's up?"

"Meet me at the back of the club with a change of clothes for Lorraine, a towel, and a hosepipe."

"What the bloody heck happened?" asked McMatters.

"Not over the phone. I'll be back soon," said Jarvis.

Lorraine, the usually mild-mannered and soft-spoken woman, had now found herself entangled in a rather precarious situation that was unimaginable to those who knew her well. The image of Lorraine as a demure and gentle individual stood in sharp contrast to the shocking reality she faced; after all, murder was hardly the kind of hobby one pursued for entertainment purposes or casual intrigue. Jarvis couldn't help but ponder how she was coping with the aftermath of her recent actions, which seemed to weigh heavily upon her like an insurmountable burden. The stark dichotomy between Lorraine's typically reserved demeanour, and the gravity of her recent actions left Jarvis utterly perplexed. How could someone so unassuming be capable of such an unspeakable deed? He found himself wondering just how she was managing to navigate the tumultuous emotional landscape, that must have emerged because of her actions. Did guilt gnaw at her insides like a ravenous beast, or had she somehow managed to compartmentalise this dark chapter within herself?

There truly was something enigmatic about Lorraine; a hidden depth that Jarvis knew lay deeply buried beneath layers of polite conversation and genteel behaviour. With this shocking revelation now surfacing, awakening aspects of her persona that had long been dormant, he couldn't help but question what else might be lurking beneath her composed exterior. What other secrets might they uncover about Lorraine, what capabilities or past transgressions would come to light as they delved deeper into her psyche? This unsettling inquiry lingered in Jarvis's mind like an unshakable shadow, casting doubt on everything he thought he understood about this once ordinary woman now shrouded in mystery and darkness.

McMatters and Lorraine really were like two peas in a pod.

Rear of the Club

Jarvis navigated the car back towards the club, the air inside was thick with an uncomfortable silence. Lorraine sat there, uncharacteristically quiet, almost as if she had been struck dumb. Unfortunately, this wasn't the first time Jarvis had witnessed her in such a state of stunned bewilderment. As they pulled up behind the club, Jarvis had to go the extra mile and get out of the vehicle to open the door for Lorraine. It was as if her normally agile limbs had suddenly turned to stone, rendering her utterly immobile. Jarvis knew it was certainly going to be an interesting debrief once they made it inside. Jarvis had learned the hard way that there was one cardinal rule everyone in the known universe was wise to abide by: never, under any circumstances, incur the wrath of the formidable Lorraine.

Jarvis was glad he got to see first-hand what Lorraine could do, now he knew how she operated and how far she could go. A cautionary tale that would undoubtedly go down in history and spread like wildfire across the digital realm, ensuring no one in their right mind would ever dare challenge the mighty Lorraine again. Jarvis knew from this moment onwards, that Lorraine was making a name for herself.

McMatters arrived on the scene, fully equipped with all the necessary supplies he believed he would need to tackle whatever situation lay ahead. His mind buzzed with thoughts of how he would face the challenges that awaited him, but nothing could have prepared him for what awaited him at the back of the club. As he stepped in sight, a sudden wave of confusion washed over him.

He came to an abrupt halt when his gaze fell upon Lorraine. Earlier that day, she had left the office clad in her new suit, a vibrant ensemble that exuded professionalism and confidence. She had looked perfectly fine and ready to conquer her tasks, radiating a sense of empowerment that seemed to uplift everyone around her. Yet now, she had returned in a state that was nothing short of shocking and heart-wrenching. The sight before him was gruesome; blood splattered everywhere, like macabre paint on an artist's canvas, creating a jarring contrast to the calm and composed way she had departed just hours previously.

The once pristine fabric of her suit bore witness to a violent encounter, now marred by dark stains that told a harrowing story of chaos and distress. It was as if each drop spoke volumes about the fear and turmoil she must have faced. McMatters struggled to reconcile this horrific scene with the image of Lorraine he had held in his mind only moments before, an image filled with hope and determination. The stark reality hit him like a bad dream that had decided to throw a surprise party in his living room; it was bizarrely surreal yet annoyingly real at the same time. An overwhelming sense of urgency gripped his heart as dread seeped into his bones, filling him with anxiety as he realized that everything had changed in an instant, not just for Lorraine, but for everyone involved in this.

The air around him became heavy with unspoken fears as McMatters took tentative steps forward, desperately trying to process what had happened, while simultaneously wishing he could turn back time or somehow restore Lorraine's dignity amidst such chaos. The stark reality unfolded around him like a chilling nightmare come to life, filling him with an overwhelming sense of urgency and dread as he realised that everything had changed in an instant.
He guided her into a humble little hut, where to her surprise, a shower had been installed. Without hesitation, he began undressing her, carefully removing every article of clothing until she stood there before him, bare and vulnerable. Wasting no time, he placed her gently under the warm cascade of water, methodically

scrubbing away every trace of the crimson stains that had previously marred her appearance.

Lorraine then cleaned the weapon that she liked a lot, her features had regained their normal, unperturbed look. McMatters, ever the dutiful lover, gathered up her discarded garments and unceremoniously stuffed them into a plastic bag, ensuring a tidy departure from the hut. Lorraine and McMatters left the hut. As they skedaddled out of the building, Jarvis found himself face-to-face with a conga line of dishevelled dudes, all itching to scrub off their impromptu ketchup costumes, all the result of Lorraine's handy work. McMatters couldn't help but gawk at the walking crime scenes, their once dapper duds now looking like they'd lost a fight with a possessed paintball gun.

It was as if these poor schmucks had accidentally wandered into a vampire's smoothie blender, emerging as living, breathing modern art installations. Their crisp shirts and ties? More like a toddler's finger-painting masterpiece. If the toddler had an unhealthy obsession with the colour red. McMatters, was eagerly awaiting the juicy details of how this whole situation had unfolded. They whispered a lot, either way McMatters was ready to feast on every crumb of gossip, after all, a little excitement was just the seasoning their otherwise monotonous workday needed.

As Jarvis, Lorraine, and McMatters approached the back entrance of the club, the door suddenly swung open with unexpected force. Lorraine barely had a moment to register the sight of Karen charging towards her, shrieking at the top of her lungs. Before the bodyguards could even react, Lorraine's lightening quick reflexes took over. Lorraine still had hold of the knife she had used earlier. Lorraine points blankly refused to let it go of it when she was being showered, Lorraine pulled the knife from her pocket and with as much force as she could muster, Lorraine threw the knife at Karen, Lorraine didn't expect that she would hit her target, but Lorraine's knife was now lodged squarely in the centre of Karen's forehead, a truly remarkable shot that left everyone in stunned silence.

The group couldn't help but be slightly amused by Lorraine's lightning-fast precision, even as they grappled with the gravity of the situation unfolding before their eyes. Everyone turned to face Lorraine, then turned and looked at the lifeless body now on the floor with a blade in her forehead. It was like they were struggling to understand how Lorraine had pulled it off.

Lorraine strode over to the blade, her eyes narrowing with determination. Lorraine pulled it from Karen's forehead by putting her foot on Karens face, then twisting and pulling as hard as she could.

"Finders keepers," she muttered under her breath, a mischievous grin spreading across her face as she scooped up the shiny, sharp object. "This baby's mine now," Lorraine declared, "Anyone got a tissue? It got a little dirty," said Lorraine. "No? Oh well."

Lorraine bent down and wiped it on Karen's clothes, stood, then walked into the club. No one was going to be prying this blade from her grasp anytime soon.

"What on earth happened today?" asked McMatters.

It wasn't a question, more a confused statement. McMatters had seen a transformation in Lorraine that had clearly shaken everyone today, he couldn't wait to hear all about it.

Jarvis turned to his men. "Can someone clean this up?"

Updating McMatters

Lorraine just couldn't shake the feeling of uncleanliness, so before proceeding with their plans, the ever-considerate McMatters insisted on taking her back to his place for a quick freshening up. After all, Lorraine was desperate to avoid returning home and facing her mother's entertaining antics in her current state. McMatters, ever the gracious and perceptive fellow, recognized the precarious predicament at hand. With a warm smile and a gentle nod, he gallantly extended an invitation for Lorraine to take refuge in his own humble abode. This sanctuary would provide her the much-needed respite to regroup, recollect her thoughts, and regain her composure before venturing forth and returning to the lively establishment.

After their revitalizing shower, Lorraine and McMatters hastily made their way back to the club. Wasting absolutely no time, Lorraine immediately poured herself a gloriously hefty serving of her signature cocktail. She proceeded to swiftly and unceremoniously chug it down in a single, decisive, and rather unladylike motion. At this point McMatters hadn't heard a dickie bird about what had happened. With a satisfied smack of her lips, she let out a delighted sigh, her eyes sparkling with mischief as she prepared to dive headfirst into the next round. This made McMatters question how bad did things get for Lorraine's well-being, as she had clearly worked up quite a thirst during the activity.

"Well, what happened?" asked McMatters.

"I will start," said Jarvis. "As you know, we found the stash house. We organized with the other families to each have a set number of men attend. All turned up itching for action." Jarvis downed his drink. "We surrounded the house and moved in sync. It worked well.

I kicked in the front door, and Bennett kicked in the back. Once inside, we quickly surrounded the three who were watching the house, tied them up, and placed them in the centre of the room."

"Jarvis gave me the nod so I could take over. I didn't have a clue what I would do or how I would do it. I asked for them all to be stripped naked and then forced to stand up. One of the Bennetts had a rather fancy looking knife that caught my eye. Unable to resist the temptation, I decided to give it a few playful twirls." Jarvis choked whilst she spoke. "Whilst twirling I may have gotten a tad careless. This resulted in some slicing and dicing here and there... redecorated the surrounding a bit." said Lorraine, and Jarvis choked again.

Lorraine downed her drink. "I asked where their boss was. One had a foul mouth, so he had to have it. I asked the next one; he wasn't nice either, so he had to have it too."

"So, you?" asked McMatters, wondering did Lorraine kill someone.

"The first man, initially his private parts slashed off, then his throat cut. The second was stabbed repeatedly. The second had a bad mouth, so that's when the painting started, and the third cried non-stop. He wet himself before Lorraine even started, but in the end, we got a location for the Slaters," said Jarvis.

McMatters stood there, his mental circuits whirring, as he attempted to comprehend the shocking revelation, that Lorraine not only appeared to have no qualms about carrying out the task at hand but was also masterful in her performance. Where had that come from?

"Steve," said Jarvis, "the thing that scared them wasn't what Lorraine did, but how she went about doing it. That really frightened them, but it also showed all the families it's not just me and you they have to worry about if they cross us. Lorraine showed that she is no pushover and will do what's needed."

"Honey, are you okay?" asked McMatters.

"Oh yes, I feel odd, but I'm okay. I had fun," said Lorraine.

All three burst out in a fit of raucous laughter at the sheer absurdity of the situation. McMatters was relieved to see that Lorraine didn't seem to have issues grappling with the fact that she had taken a life, which led him to ponder whether this was her first rodeo, or if she had, in fact, been a secret serial killer all along, masterfully covering her tracks until now. The mental image of prim and proper Lorraine, the epitome of innocence and propriety, nonchalantly adding yet another gruesome trophy to her proverbial "murder belt" was simply too much for the group to handle. Dissolving into fits of uncontrollable laughter, they found themselves doubled over, tears of mirth streaming down their reddened faces as they desperately gasped for air, the sheer absurdity of the mental picture leaving them in stitches and utterly unable to compose themselves.

Chapter Twenty-Eight
Location, Location, Location

The Santos obtained the address from a distraught man whom they felt sympathy for, so they paid him to remain silent and leave town. The Santos made it clear that no harm would come to him if he complied but warned that if he tried to warn the Slater boss, he would face the wrath and retribution of the families involved. This coercive tactic was employed to ensure the man's cooperation and prevent him from interfering with their plans, which likely involved some nefarious activities targeting the Slater organization. The Santos boss had now obtained the location of the Slater boss. However, before taking any further action, Santos needed to confirm that the Slaters were indeed present at the specified location. To do this, the Santos team decided to conduct a stakeout and closely monitor the target site to verify the Slaters' presence and activities. By carefully observing the location, Santos could gather the necessary intelligence to determine their next steps and plan their approach accordingly.

The Slaters found themselves taking refuge in an old, shuttered bookstore that had been forced to close its doors five years earlier. This closure was largely attributed to the shift towards online book purchasing, and the intense competition from large supermarket chains, which had undercut the profit margins of traditional, brick and mortar bookshops. While the exterior of the abandoned store showed some signs of neglect, the overall condition was not too severe. Meanwhile, Santos had positioned another team at the front of the building, while he himself had moved to the rear, ensuring a coordinated approach to the operation. Upon speaking with the distraught man, Santos learned that there are only a small number of Slater's crew members left, no more than ten. The group no longer has a defined organizational structure or specialized roles, and they lack established connections within the drug trade. Instead, they subsist by stealing shipments from other criminal organizations and reselling the contraband. The boss of the Slaters crew, while lacking in many skills, does possess the ability to carry out explosive attacks, which ironically has made the group's illicit operations somewhat easier to execute.... This made Santos laugh, as they were just wannabes. Santos phoned McMatters.

"Hey McMatters, it's Santos."

"Hi, how's things?"

"That woman of yours... boy! Does she know how to scare the shit out of others or what! I like the way she did it, though, I must say."

"Thanks, I'll pass it on, Santos. Did you get the address?"

"Yep, we're sat on it and watching."

"Where are they?"

"The old bookstore in town. A bit too public to grab from the front quietly anyway, but I can keep watching. He'll have to move at some point."

"Thanks, Santos. I'll get one of my guys to come up and sit back, and a Bennett on the front. Frees you up a bit."

"Thanks, no problem. Speak soon."

McMatters is willing to play the long game and exercise patience, but the constant annoyance posed by the Slaters is beginning to wear on him. A part of him harbours the urge to lash out and tear the place apart, as the relentless aggravation is testing his resolve. However, McMatters recognizes that a measured, deliberate approach is more prudent in this situation. He knows that slow and steady progress, rather than rash actions, will ultimately serve him better in the long run. McMatters also took onboard the words about Lorraine, and how she scared the shit out of everyone. McMatters thought this was impressive.

"That was Santos, it seems you made an impression Lorraine!" said McMatters.

"I can't think why," said Lorraine coyly.

"He's watching the old bookstore in town, where they are holed up. We will send a guy to watch from a distance, and a Bennett to watch the front. Make it clear though, no touching" said McMatters.

"Yep, on it," said Jarvis.

Bennetts

McMatters knew that a call with the Bennetts' leader was an absolute necessity. It was his job, after all, to ensure that everything ran as smoothly as a well-oiled machine. He couldn't help but wonder if they too, would bring up the topic of Lorraine. So far, it seemed like there was a bit more to the story than what had been disclosed, and he was dying to get to the bottom of it.

"Bennett, how are you?" asked McMatters.

"McMatters, hey! I'm good, thanks. Now that I've showered all of the red away."

"That much blood then?"

"Yes indeed. It was good to see she can carry her own, not just some arm candy."

"Very true, Bennett. Very true. I know Jarvis just got you to send someone to watch the front of the bookstore."

"Yes, he has. He's very efficient."

"Tell me about it. One other thing: Lorraine said it was one of your blades she used."

"Yes, it was."

"I'm not sure you're going to get it back. She appears to have grown attached to it."

"Don't worry. Tell her it's my gift for doing an amazing job."

"Will do. Speak soon."

"Okay, bye."

McMatters gazed at Lorraine, flashing a self-assured, grin.

"Well, well, looks like you've managed to work your charm on them as well, haven't you?" he remarked, his tone dripping with a hint of playful jest.

Clearly, Lorraine's captivating presence had once again worked its magic, winning over the hearts and minds of their unsuspecting crime bosses.

"What did he say about my new toy?" asked Lorraine.

"It's his gift to you for such a well-done job."

Lorraine smiled at the thought that she had accomplished what needed to be done. She was no fool; she understood the unspoken expectations that accompanied her position, especially whilst under the scrutiny of the other families. If she were to stand in front of them, it was imperative that she demonstrated her ability to assert herself, and command respect. She had to show them that she could kick arse, hold her own, and above all, not back down in the face of adversity. Reflecting on this moment filled her with a sense of satisfaction, as Lorraine realised that not only had she successfully made her point known, but she had also instilled a sense of apprehension in them, a quiet fear that would linger long after their encounter. It was crucial for her to establish boundaries, and convey the clear message, that any attempts at undermining or challenging her authority would be met with fierce resistance. In this way, Lorraine felt empowered; by standing firm and exhibiting strength, she had ensured that they would think twice before ever considering any form of disrespect, or challenge to her authority in the future.

Blythe

As Blythe's handler, Lorraine had to make the critical call about the Slaters. McMatters and Jarvis had teams from each family positioned and ready, keeping a close eye on the bookstore, eagerly anticipating the moment when the Slaters would make a move, that would leave them vulnerable. It was a tense standoff, with both sides poised to pounce at the first sign of weakness from their rivals. Lorraine knew she had to time her decision perfectly, lest the whole delicate operation unravel in spectacular fashion.

"Blythe, we have a location. We need one of your team to join the watch party."

"Hello, Lorraine. Yes, we can't wait for some revenge. Where are they?"

"Remember, no moving without us. Just wait and watch with the others for now. We are all waiting and watching the old bookstore in town. It's too populated to hit there, but we will wait for them to leave, so we will have a good place to strike."

"I understand, Lorraine. Thank you. I will send someone to watch."

"Thank you, will speak later, Blythe."

Lorraine was growing increasingly worried that Blythe might take matters into his own hands. After all, it was his shipment that had been hit, and his men who had been hospitalised as a result. Blythe was not known for his patience, or forgiving nature, and Lorraine could practically hear the gears turning in his head, as he contemplated retaliatory action. She braced herself for the potential fallout, hoping against hope that Blythe would exercise some restraint and not do anything rash. But knowing him, Lorraine wouldn't be surprised if he decided to take the law into his own hands and dish out a little street justice of his own. This was bound to get messy, and she just hoped she wouldn't get caught in the crossfire.

Chapter Twenty-Nine
McMatters' Place

It was well past two in the morning when McMatters finally decided it was time to call it a night. The long, arduous day had taken its toll, and it was clear that everyone, especially Lorraine, were in dire need of some rest.

"Alright, you lot," McMatters addressing them all.

"Time to hit the sack. I suggest you get some shut eye while you can, eh Jarvis?" Jarvis readily agreed.

Lorraine, energy reserves now thoroughly depleted, simply gathered her belongings and quietly made her way towards the exit, foregoing any further small talk. The day's events had clearly drained her, and she was eager to find the solace of sleep. With gentle understanding, McMatters noticed Lorraine's overwhelming exhaustion as they arrived at his place. Seeing her struggle to stand, he kindly assisted her up the stairs, offering support every step of the way. Once Lorraine entered the bedroom, the profound exhaustion she felt caused her to collapse onto the bed, where even the simple task of removing her shoes appeared to be an overwhelming challenge. Recognizing Lorraine's state of physical and emotional depletion, McMatters approached her with a compassionate demeanour, tenderly coming to her aid. With the utmost respect and consideration, McMatters carefully helped Lorraine undress, providing the gentle support and care she so desperately needed in that moment. With the utmost care and tenderness, he gently helped her settle into the soft, inviting comfort of the bed. Ensuring her body was supported and her mind could find solace, he meticulously adjusted the bedding to provide the warmth and security she needed to finally allow her weary form to relax and her restless thoughts to subside. In this quiet, peaceful moment, he conveyed his heartfelt compassion, creating a soothing environment where she could find the respite her body and soul so desperately craved. With a heavy heart, McMatters poured himself a sombre drink, his mind weighed down by the tragic events that had unfolded throughout the day.

He couldn't help but feel a profound sense of sorrow and empathy for the lives that had been lost, and the immense pain that had been inflicted. Lorraine's actions, though undoubtedly shell shocking, also spoke of a drive within her, which propelled her whilst she was carrying out such extreme measures. McMatters recognized the complex emotions and underlying anguish that must have compelled her, and he found himself grappling with a mix of worry and concern. The violent deaths of those men from what the families had said, Lorraine performed very well, and a lesson was given on a new style of punishment. Then there was Karen, his ex. Despite their past, he never wished such a fate upon her. But Karen had lied, stolen and cheated her way through life, so this outcome would have caught up with her eventually.

The unexpected passing of Karen, was in some ways, not entirely surprising given the circumstances surrounding her demise. As McMatters sipped his drink, he found himself overcome with a profound sense of compassion. He couldn't help but feel deeply for Lorraine and hoped that the immense pain and anguish of this experience would not leave her permanently scarred or diminish her spirit in the long run. McMatters knew Karen had it coming, after all she had done. It had hurt McMatters when Karen said he had a child. After he wrapped his head around it and got used to the idea, it turned out that he didn't; it was another of Karen's lies to get money from him. This had hit him hard. He had liked the idea of being a dad. McMatters found himself filled with a sense of awe and wonder as he contemplated the possibility of discussing his deepest feelings with Lorraine. The two had grown increasingly close, and McMatters couldn't help but wonder if Lorraine had ever considered the prospect of starting a family.

The thought of taking their relationship to the next level, and potentially welcoming children into their lives filled McMatters' heart with a mixture of hope and trepidation. He yearned to know if Lorraine shared his dreams of building a life and a family together, yet he was also acutely aware of the intensity of such a conversation. McMatters knew that broaching this topic could potentially reshape the very foundation of their relationship, and he found himself grappling with the weight of the decision he found before him. As McMatters quietly climbed into bed, he gazed in awe at the sleeping form of his beloved Lorraine. In that peaceful moment, he couldn't help but marvel at just how truly beautiful she was, a vision of radiant, serene perfection that took his breath away. McMatters felt a profound sense of gratitude and wonder, knowing that this remarkable woman was his to cherish. Lorraine's recent growth, and the development of her remarkable skills did not concern McMatters in the slightest. If anything, it only served to deepen his appreciation and admiration for her. In his eyes, they were kindred spirits, two peas in a pod, perfectly matched and attuned to one another. McMatters knew, without a doubt, that he was the luckiest man alive, to have Lorraine in his life.

In the morning, Lorraine awoke in a state of bewilderment, her mind completely devoid of any recollection of how she had arrived at Steve's place, or the events that had transpired thereafter. As she stirred from her slumber, she found herself in McMatters' bedroom, her clothes neatly folded beside the bed, leaving her utterly perplexed and disoriented by the mysterious circumstances surrounding her current situation. The sheer blankness of her memory, only served to heighten her sense of awe and disbelief at the unexplained turn of events that had unfolded.

Not long after McMatters slowly roused from his slumber, he became acutely aware of Lorraine's captivating gaze fixed intently upon him as she watched him sleep. The sensation of her eyes carefully observing his peaceful, resting form filled him with a profound sense of wonder and reverence. McMatters found himself transfixed, almost mesmerized, by Lorraine's unwavering attention, her gentle presence casting an air of reverence over the tranquil scene. In that moment, he felt a deep, almost mystical connection, as if Lorraine's watchful eyes held the power to glimpse into the very depths of his soul while he lay vulnerable in his unconscious state.

"Lorraine, can we talk for a short while please?"

"Yes, we can indeed."

"Last night I was processing something, and my mind wandered over possibilities, but I don't know how you think or feel on the subject."

"Ask away."

"When Karen told me that I had a child, my mind reeled. I didn't know how I felt, but eventually I got used to the idea, and quite liked the thought of having a child and being called dad."

"Have you ever wanted or thought about having children?"

"I have. I always dreamed of having them, but it was never the right moment, and I always said I'd never bring children up the way I was."

"You said 'children'. Do you see more than one child?"

"One is lonely, three is too many, one always gets left out, but two is a good number."

"Have you thought of us having children?"

"I've dreamed about it a few times, I must admit."

"Will... could we? I mean, I know I'm getting excited here for a second, but will you have a child with me?"

"Yes, I would love to."

"Oh my God! We are going to have a child or two! Woohoo! You have made me so happy!"

"I have something to tell you Steve" Steve's eyes went wide. "I love you Mr McMatters"

Lorraine felt a surge of excitement and desire wash over her. As she tentatively slid her hand beneath the soft, plush blankets, she was thrilled to discover that he was eagerly anticipating her touch, his body primed and receptive to her caresses. The electricity of their mutual anticipation filled the air, heightening the sensations and making Lorraine's heart race with giddy, breathless anticipation. Lorraine and McMatters spent most of the morning engaged in a passionate, electrifying, and utterly captivating intimate encounter. Their lovemaking was nothing short of mind-bogglingly intense and exhilarating, leaving them both breathless and utterly satiated. The raw, primal energy and sheer physical ecstasy they experienced together was truly awe-inspiring, transcending the purely physical realm and tapping into a deeper, more profound connection. Their bodies moved to a perfect, harmonious rhythm, as if guided by an ancient, instinctual dance, culminating in waves of earth-shattering pleasure, that left them both trembling with the afterglow of their incredible shared experience.

"Steve, I need to nip home. I've no clean clothes here; I used the spare office set yesterday."

"Move in with me."

"Really? Just like that?"

"Yes. We're going to be starting a new life together, and it's not right if we're apart."

"Okay, I see. Yes, in that case I will move in."

McMatters abruptly leapt out of bed, his eyes wild and his expression contorted with unbridled love. Overcome by intense, irrational feelings, he lets out a thunderous shout that echoes throughout the room: "Wooohooo!" His voice is laced with a palpable mixture of mania and happiness.

"I guess mum will be happy. She has my place to herself!"

Chapter Thirty
Lorraine's Place

Both Lorraine and Steve arrive at Lorraine's house, their faces beaming with a sense of awe and unbridled joy. As they reach their destination, they are greeted by the unexpected presence of Demetrio, who appears to have remained there throughout the night. The radiant expressions on Lorraine and Steve's faces convey a palpable excitement and wonder at the unfolding events, hinting at the profound significance or remarkable nature of their encounter with Demetrio, and the circumstances that led him to stay the night.

"Mum, Demetrio, good morning," said Lorraine.

"Hi Demetrio, good night, was it?" asked McMatters.

"Wonderful, absolutely wonderful. The meal was fantastic, the dancing, it was all wonderful," said Demetrio.

"Oh, hello Lorraine, are you stopping?"

"Mum, come sit for a minute. I need to talk to you."

Maxine sat down on the edge of a chair, her expression etched with a deep sense of worry and unease. The tense line of her brow and the slight trembling of her hands betrayed the inner turmoil, that had gripped her at that moment. She perched precariously on the chair's edge, as if ready to spring into action at the slightest provocation, her body language conveying a palpable tension and apprehension. Maxine's typically calm and composed demeanour had given way to a palpable aura of distress, hinting at concerns, that were weighing heavily on her mind.

"Mum. I'm moving in with Steve. Don't worry though, you can stay here," said Lorraine.

"I won't see you as much Lorraine."

"Yes, you will. I will make sure of it, Mum."

"So, I get this place to myself?"

"Yes, Mum, and we can swap things around upstairs so that you get the bigger room."

"Oh, that would be fantastic, Lorraine!"

"That settles it then," said Lorraine. She got up and went upstairs to grab some clean clothes.

"I will come back later on, to grab my things mum." Lorraine shouts downstairs so she can be heard.

"OK Steve, let's go."

"I will look after this place," said Maxine.

Maxine

"Maxine... last night was fantastic!" said Demetrio.

"The energy, the passion, the meal and we can't forget the desert. It was truly a breath-taking experience, that left me in awe. Next time though, why don't we host at my place? I'd love to have you over. We can make a whole evening of it. I would make dinner beforehand, then we could unwind. I hope you'll strongly consider it, as I would be honoured to share such a memorable evening in the company of someone who clearly appreciates it, as much as I do".

"I would love that, Demetrio. It sounds wonderful. Thank you for a remarkable night."

Demetrio, with the kind of charm that could make even a cat video look boring, leans in and plants a soft, delicate kiss on each of Maxine's cheeks, like he's auditioning for a romantic role in a blockbuster film. It's the sort of gesture that makes you wonder if he's been practicing in front of a mirror, or if he just knows how to turn ordinary moments into cinematic magic. After this intimate display that would make Cupid, himself shed a proud tear, he spins around and struts away like he just won an Oscar for 'Best Kiss'.

Maxine is left standing there, her cheeks resembling ripe tomatoes, and her heart performing somersaults worthy of an Olympic gymnast. She's utterly captivated, standing in what can only be described as an awestruck daze, wondering if she has just stepped into a scene from one of those sappy romance novels she secretly loves to read.

Chapter Thirty-one
The Club

Jarvis arrives at the club earlier than usual, feeling a growing sense of unease. He was concerned that in the aftermath of the previous day's events, the staff may not have thoroughly cleaned up all the traces of blood from the exterior hut. The thought of lingering evidence of the incident, weighed heavily on his mind as he approached the premises, unsure of what he might find. Jarvis knew he needed to exercise caution and discretion, as any overlooked details could potentially pose a serious risk, or complications going forward. Just in case, Jarvis decides to summon Eric to inspect the premises, it is crucial to ensure that the area is thoroughly cleaned and free of any incriminating evidence. The presence of Jarvis, a potentially suspicious individual, raises concerns about the need for heightened vigilance and attention to detail. It is essential to meticulously scour the space, leaving no trace of any activities, or materials that could be deemed questionable or compromising. Maintaining a clean and evidence-free environment is paramount in this situation, as it could have serious implications if discovered by the watchful Jarvis.

"Eric, I have a job for you," said Jarvis.

"Ahhh... Jarvis! No problem... give me thirty minutes I will be there."

"Thanks Eric."
When Eric arrived, he was shown all the areas to be cleaned. Jarvis's car, the back of the club, in the yard, and the hut. All needed a splatter check and cleaning. Eric and his team got to work. By the time they had finished, it was all like new. Eric was leaving just as McMatters and Lorraine arrived.

"Good morning, how are we all feeling today?" asked Jarvis.

"I'm pretty good, but in need of a good coffee though," said Lorraine.

"I feel good, Jarvis. Real good."

"Oh, do I dare ask why?"

"Lorraine is moving in with me," said McMatters.

"Oh wow, congratulations! That's fantastic," said Jarvis.

"Any updates on the Slaters?" asked McMatters.

"Not as yet, but they can't stay in that building forever. At some point, they will need to come out," said Jarvis wondering if it would work.

"Well, if they don't soon, I might have to make them come out," said Lorraine, who was getting impatient.

"I'm all ears on how we could do that," McMatters said.

"When they can't stand the heat, they'll get out of the kitchen. Or in this case, a bookshop," Jarvis replied.

"I mean, we could force them to exit," he added.

"Let's see what happens tonight. If there's no movement, we'll try smoking them out," said McMatters.

Lorraine found herself in uncharted territory, both exhilarated and apprehensive about all the significant changes, that were unfolding in her life. Moving in with Steve was a major milestone, that she had never experienced with any previous romantic partner, signalling a profound shift in the trajectory of their relationship. Moreover, the couple's discussion about having children together, evoked a mixture of excitement and trepidation within Lorraine. While the prospect of building a family with Steve was a long-held desire for Lorraine, the idea also brought a sense of unease.

The commitment and responsibility that comes with parenthood can be daunting, even for those who have yearned for it. Lorraine found herself grappling with the weight of these decisions, aware that the choices she and Steve made would profoundly shape their shared future. Navigating this transitional phase, Lorraine felt a surge of vitality, but also recognized the inherent risks and uncertainties that accompanied such significant life changes.

The path forwards, though thrilling, was also tinged with a degree of trepidation as she contemplated the implications of her new living arrangements, and the potential for starting a family with Steve. Recently, other aspects of Lorraine's behaviour and demeanour had undergone noticeable changes as well. While Lorraine had always exuded a sense of confidence, she had not traditionally been perceived as overtly brash or domineering. In the past, Lorraine had maintained a level of control, meting out disciplinary measures, when necessary, but not to the extent that had become increasingly apparent of late. This recent shift in Lorraine's approach is quite striking, serving as a potential eye-opener. Worryingly, Lorraine appears to have developed a newfound enjoyment in doling out punishment, a development that does not seem to evoke any feelings of apprehension or concern within her. This lack of unease regarding her own punitive tendencies, could be a cause for alarm, as it suggests a concerning evolution in Lorraine's mind set and behavioural patterns.

The prospect of balancing the demanding role of a mafia boss with the responsibilities of parenting, raises some significant concerns. Lorraine would face an immense challenge in trying to reconcile these two vastly different and often conflicting identities. The high-stakes, cutthroat nature of organized crime is inherently at odds with the nurturing, protective instincts required of an effective parent. Maintaining the ruthlessness and single-minded focus needed to succeed in the mafia world, while also providing the love, guidance, and stability a child requires, would place an extraordinary strain on Lorraine, potentially compromising her ability to excel in either realm.

The question remains whether Lorraine possesses the exceptional skills, and unwavering discipline necessary to effectively navigate these two vastly divergent spheres, without compromising her integrity or the wellbeing of her family. Lorraine was abruptly jolted back to the present as a sudden, startling noise erupted directly in front of her. The unexpected sound, loud and jarring, instantly pulled her focus away from her thoughts and forced her to re-engage with her immediate surroundings. This sudden disruption caused Lorraine to become acutely aware of her environment again, breaking the trance-like state, she had previously been in. The loud noise that had manifested right before her face demanded her full, undivided attention, effectively snapping her out of her distracted, inward-facing mindset.

"Ah, you are back with us again," McMatters grinned.

"As it's quiet at the moment, why don't you go and start packing up the things that you need to bring to mine later?" said McMatters.

"Yes, I guess I could make a start. Would you phone me if I'm needed, please?"

"Of course we will," said McMatters.

Lorraine hurried to call for her personal driver, eager to depart the premises as soon as possible. Feeling a growing sense of excitement, she quickly made her way down to the building's main entrance, her steps quickening with each passing moment. Lorraine's desire to leave the location was palpable, hinting at an underlying happiness that prompted her rushed exit. McMatters found himself alone in the office with Jarvis, providing an opportunity to engage in more open and unrestrained conversation now that Lorraine had departed. This private setting allowed them to discuss matters more freely, without the potential constraints or inhibitions, that Lorraine's presence may have imposed. With Lorraine no longer there, McMatters and Jarvis could now speak more candidly and explore topics in a greater depth, away from any external scrutiny or influence.

"It's a big thing you both moving in together. How do you feel?" asked Jarvis.

"Really good. I'm excited and happy for the first time in that long, that I had forgotten what it felt like," said McMatters.

"That's great to hear. I am pleased for you both,"

"Thanks mate. I know you look out for me. Me and Lorraine had a real deep conversation and found out what we both wanted."

"It's good to know what you both want, and if it's the same thing, who knows how far it will go?" said Jarvis.

"Let's have a drink to you and Lorraine?"

Jarvis carefully poured two generous drinks, the amber liquid swirling in the glasses as he handed one to his companion. They leaned back in their chairs, the sound of the glasses gently clinking together as they raised their drinks and exchanged a solemn "cheers." The simple act belied the underlying tension in the air, a cautious acknowledgment of the gravity of the situation they now found themselves in.

"As soon as this business with the Slaters is finished, we should all sit down for a big meal and have a celebration." said McMatters.

"Yes, a great idea. We haven't done that in a long time," said Jarvis.

McMatters' thoughts drifted back to that last meal everyone had shared. A gathering that lingered in his memory for a multitude of reasons. Among the attendees, he recalled the laughter and conversations that had filled the air. However, one detail stood out vividly: Karen would not be attending this time around. He felt a sense of relief wash over him, knowing that her presence had previously cast a shadow over what should have been an enjoyable evening, turning it into a tense affair filled with uncomfortable moments. The last supper had included an eclectic mix of personalities. Jarvis with his boisterous stories, Paulie always ready with a quick joke, and Mike's calm demeanour providing balance amidst the chaos. The security teams were present as well; their vigilant eyes scanning the room for any signs of trouble while ensuring everyone felt safe.

The heads of each family were there too, seated at the table like esteemed dignitaries at a state dinner, flanked by their closest associates who whispered secrets and shared insider knowledge. As he reminisced about that previous gathering, McMatters estimated there were perhaps twenty-two or twenty-five people gathered around that table. Yet this time promised to be even more significant, a much larger assembly, where alliances could be forged, and old rivalries might resurface in unexpected ways. He pondered on who else might join them this time around. New faces bringing fresh dynamics, or old acquaintances rehashing familiar grievances, and how these interactions would shape the atmosphere of their upcoming meal.

This upcoming meal would encompass a diverse and rather large gathering, featuring key individuals such as McMatters, Lorraine, Jarvis, Paulie, Mike, Bennett and Santos who stand out as two of the primary leaders of the new assembly. In addition to these pivotal figures, there would be other attendees added to the mix. Santos is expected to bring along three companions, adding further depth to the gathering. Reflecting on the security aspect of the event reveals that the family has expanded considerably. It has grown to accommodate a total of sixteen members dedicated solely to ensuring the safety and smooth operations, during this significant occasion. Moreover, we cannot overlook the Blythe's.

They will contribute another three individuals to the ranks. When we tally everyone up for this function, we find ourselves counting thirty-one participants in total. However, lest we forget, Maxine and Demetrio two important figures whose presence will undoubtedly enhance the atmosphere, that brings our count to a noteworthy thirty-three attendees. It is with hopeful anticipation, that McMatters considers whether Demetrio's venue will be able to host such a sizable gathering comfortably; he plans to reach out soon for confirmation regarding logistical details. This thoughtful approach underscores not only the importance of gathering these influential individuals' togetherness, but also highlights McMatters' commitment to ensuring that every aspect of this meal is perfectly orchestrated for both productivity and camaraderie.

McMatters reflects on the tasks that lie ahead, particularly the important responsibility of assisting Lorraine in retrieving her belongings from her house. He envisions a practical strategy: utilizing Lorraine's dedicated security team to facilitate the entire process of moving her possessions. This team, composed of capable and robust individuals, brings an invaluable resource to the table. Their strength and expertise will not only make the logistics easier but will also ensure that everything is handled with care and efficiency. Once they have successfully relocated Lorraine's items, McMatters considers how they can further assist by helping Maxine transition into what was once Lorraine's old room.

This plan not only serves a functional purpose but also symbolizes a new beginning for Maxine within those familiar walls. After all, there's a certain irony in having such big, strong men at one's disposal; their potential becomes wasted if not harnessed when the situation calls for it. In this case, McMatters recognizes that their assistance is not just beneficial, it's essential for making this transition smooth and seamless. Jarvis, with his sharp and timely intervention, jolts McMatters back to reality just as he was becoming deeply immersed in his daydream. In that fleeting moment, McMatters had been passionately contemplating the delightful idea of bestowing names upon each room in his expansive house, an imaginative endeavour he envisioned with boundless enthusiasm. This was not merely an exercise in creativity; it was a chance to breathe life into the many unexplored spaces that have laid dormant, eagerly awaiting discovery by Lorraine. Each room held its own unique potential for character and charm, and McMatters found himself utterly enchanted by the thought of crafting a narrative for every corner of his home. The notion of christening these rooms filled him with an electrifying sense of purpose and excitement, as if he were embarking on a whimsical journey to transform mundane spaces into realms brimming with stories and memories waiting to be created.

"The Slaters should come out soon. They will now be short on food and drink."

"I hope so, we have a lot on hold because of them."

"Tell me about it!"

Jarvis

Jarvis had observed a profound transformation in McMatters ever since he had started his relationship with Lorraine. This newfound connection seemed to have anchored him, instilling within him a much-needed sense of purpose, that had previously eluded him. It was as if Lorraine's presence acted like an anchor in the turbulent seas of McMatters' life, guiding him towards calmer waters and brighter horizons. However, Jarvis couldn't shake the haunting memories brought on by the aftermath of what Karen had done to McMatters, a betrayal that not only shattered his dreams, but also left deep emotional scars. McMatters had always harboured an aspiration to become a father; it was a dream he cherished deeply. Karen introduced this beautiful concept to him, filling his heart with hope and joy, only to snatch it away cruelly through one devastating lie that killed a part of McMatters' spirit deep inside. The weight of that loss loomed over him like a dark cloud, dimming his once-vibrant enthusiasm for life and fatherhood. Yet amidst this turmoil, Jarvis held onto a hope that the blossoming relationship between McMatters and Lorraine, would evolve into something far more profound and fulfilling: a family where both could realize their dreams together. They truly deserved nothing less than that radiant future, filled with love and laughter; it was time for them both to embrace happiness after so much heartache.

Jarvis fully grasped the tumultuous emotions that drove Lorraine to take the drastic step of killing Karen. In the depths of his heart, he felt a complex swirl of understanding, and even empathy for Lorraine's actions. The weight of the situation hung heavy in the air, a palpable tension that spoke of their shared struggles and pain. If he were to be completely honest with himself, he recognized a dark truth; had Lorraine not acted first, there was a twisted part of him that would have forced him to take matters into his own hands. The thought lingered like a shadow, revealing just how far desperation could push someone into moral ambiguity. This revelation left Jarvis grappling with his own sense of right and wrong, as he pondered the thin line between justice and vengeance in their chaotic world.

"Why don't you go and take some time, while we are waiting for movement on the Slaters, and help Lorraine make a start moving her stuff into your place? I will sort this place out."

"Are you sure?"

"Yep, scoot."

Chapter Thirty-Two

Detective Winters

Detective Winters had not been having a great time since she took over from Detective Jackson, a situation that weighed heavily on her shoulders. The shadows of unsolved mysteries loomed larger each day, tormenting her with relentless questions: Who killed Jackson? Who was responsible for the brutal murders of the men in the street? And most chilling of all, who transformed the Birch pub into the gruesome bloodbath, that had sent shockwaves through the community? The silence on the streets was deafening. A suffocating blanket that stifled any hope of finding answers, or garnering leads. It was as if an unspoken pact hung over the city, where fear held sway and loyalty to an unseen power suppressed any chance of the truth emerging.

This city, vibrant and bustling with life, should have been filled with voices willing to share their stories. Yet here she was, surrounded by countless witnesses rendered mute by intimidation or despair. The eerie silence deeply unsettled Detective Winters. It gnawed at her insides like an unrelenting predator stalking its prey. The realization that someone, or perhaps a group held such dominion over this vast urban landscape filled her with dread. In a city teeming with people and brimming with potential informants, why could she not find anyone willing to speak out? What kind of fear could grip an entire populace so tightly, that even whispering could mean risking their lives? This disturbing silence not only haunted her thoughts, but ignited a fierce determination within her, a fire fuelled by the desire for justice and resolution. Detective Winters knew she must peel back the layers of this chilling mystery before it consumed her entirely; each unanswered question drove her deeper into a labyrinth where shadows danced mockingly just out of reach. She would not rest until she uncovered who wielded such control over the city streets, and exposed the truth hidden beneath layers of terror and intimidation.

Today, Detective Winters will set off on a journey to a secluded house nestled in the heart of the countryside, a place where tranquillity often masked the shadows of darker secrets. A chilling report had surfaced regarding blood found at the scene, but curiously, no further details accompanied this alarming discovery. This lack of information only deepened the mystery surrounding the case, and heightened Winters' sense of urgency. Determined to unravel this enigma, she rallied her entire team to accompany her on this crucial mission. They were not just colleagues; they were comrades, bound by an unwavering commitment to uncovering the truth, whatever it may hold. As they drove through winding roads flanked by towering trees, each member felt a mix of apprehension and anticipation. What would they find upon their arrival? The hope was that this investigation would lead to something substantial that Detective Winters could take back to Sergeant Cole, a breakthrough that could illuminate the shadows lurking within this rural setting. Fingers crossed and hearts racing, they all shared one common goal: solving this case and bringing justice to where it was needed most. Each step forward was not just a step into the unknown; it was a step toward illuminating secrets, that had been hidden away in darkness for far too long.

When Detective Winters arrived at the house, she was taken aback by the profound sense of seclusion that enveloped her. Nestled atop a hill, and surrounded by fields, that had long surrendered to nature's relentless embrace, the house seemed like a forgotten relic from another era. The once meticulously tended grounds had transformed into an untamed wilderness, with wildflowers and tall grasses swaying gently in the breeze, whispering secrets of days gone by. As she surveyed her surroundings, it became apparent that no other dwelling was visible in any direction; it was as if this enigmatic abode had been deliberately hidden from the world. This isolation not only heightened her curiosity, but also sent a shiver down her spine. What mysteries awaited her within those walls? The stillness of the landscape contrasted sharply with the chaotic events that had led her there, igniting a burning determination within Winters to uncover the truth lurking beneath this tranquil facade.

The house stood in a state of disrepair, its exterior bearing the unmistakable signs of neglect and decay. With peeling paint and overgrown weeds creeping up the sides, it looked as though no one had set foot inside for at least ten to twenty years. Yet, one could not help but wonder if this dilapidation had been long in the making, perhaps lingering in a shadowy limbo even before that time. The atmosphere was heavy with an eerie silence, as if the very walls held secrets just waiting to be uncovered. As the team carefully surveyed the property from the outside, they searched for clues, or potential evidence that might provide insight into what had transpired within these crumbling walls. Their eyes scoured every corner for anything that seemed out of place, objects that appeared too new or fresh against the backdrop of decay were particularly telling.

A few unsettling observations caught their attention; notably, both the front and back doors bore clear signs of having been kicked in with force. This violent intrusion hinted at a recent disturbance, but deciphering whether it was an isolated incident or part of a longer narrative proved challenging. The mystery deepened with each passing moment, as they contemplated what stories this forlorn house might tell if only it could speak.

Detective Winters strode through the front door, her team trailing closely behind her. Each step resonating with a mix of anticipation and dread. The scene that unfolded before them was every bit as grim as she had feared. Inside, the once vibrant space had succumbed to neglect and decay; the walls, now reduced to mere planks of wood, stood precariously, many barely clinging to their frames and joists, as if in a desperate fight against gravity. The air was thick with an unsettling stillness, punctuated only by the crunch of debris underfoot. Large clumps of plaster lay scattered across the floor, like forgotten remnants of a once lively environment, having surrendered to time and disrepair. The atmosphere hung heavy with the echoes of past stories waiting to be uncovered amidst the ruin. As they entered the main room of the house downstairs, an unimaginable horror unfolded before their eyes.

The scene was drenched in blood, with a massive pool at the centre, that seemed to pulsate with a life of its own. This grotesque mound was smeared with disturbing patterns, imprints that looked eerily like those of a human posterior, accompanied by what might have been the scrape of a foot or leg. Each leaving behind a chilling mark in the crimson liquid that surrounded it. The air was thick with an acrid stench, a foul reminder of urine, that had long since dried into the wooden floorboards, mingling unsettlingly with the metallic scent of blood. Detective Winters straightened herself and took in her surroundings. Her heart raced as she noticed her team standing frozen in disbelief, their eyes wide and fixated on the walls.

These surfaces were not merely stained, but splattered wildly, with some streaks running in chaotic patterns, while others appeared as if someone had aggressively sprayed blood without restraint. Each splatter told its own terrifying story. A shudder coursed through Detective Winters as she contemplated who could have committed such an atrocity, and what nightmarish events might have previously unfolded here. The weight of despair hung heavily in her chest, as she realized that whoever had been present in this room almost certainly met with a tragic end, an end reflected vividly by the sheer volume of blood, which soaked every corner and crevice around them.

"Get the crime scene investigation team here, I'm hoping someone left something for us to find."

Chapter Thirty-Three

Lorraine's Place

Lorraine was up to her eyeballs in a veritable mountain of clothes, shoes, and bags, that seemed to multiply like rabbits every time she turned around. It was as if her wardrobe had staged a coup, determined to make packing for this trip an Olympic event. In a moment of sheer desperation, Lorraine plopped down on one of the overstuffed suitcases, striking a pose that could only be described as "bargain-bin chic," while McMatters wrestled with the zipper, as if it were a wild animal intent on escaping. The sound of the zipper straining against its fabric prison, echoed through the room like an awkward symphony. Meanwhile, Maxine stood at the door, doubled over with laughter, at this circus act that was unfolding before her, complete with Lorraine's exaggerated sighs, sitting and jumping on the suitcase, and McMatters' futile attempts at zipping it shut. It was pure comedy gold; who knew packing could be such an entertaining spectacle?

"You could help us, Mum."

"Nah, I'm having far too much fun watching you both, to help."

After what felt like an eternity of wrestling with stubborn zippers, and misbehaving accessories, Lorraine finally, triumphantly completed the daunting task of packing her clothes. It was a saga filled with dramatic moments, like the time she had to negotiate with that one particularly clingy sweater, that simply refused to fit into her suitcase. Exhausted, and slightly worn out from this epic battle against fabric and footwear, Lorraine and McMatters decided they deserved a well-earned reward.

So, they opted for a refreshing drink, to help them recover from their packing ordeal. After all, who knew packing could be so physically taxing? With glasses raised high, they toasted to their triumph over luggage chaos, laughing at the absurdity of it all, while plotting their next adventure, that hopefully required a lot less heavy lifting! With the soft stuff now done, because let's be honest, who doesn't love a good pile of cushions to wrestle with, they can finally start boxing up all the rest of the room. It's like playing Tetris, but instead of colourful blocks, it's an assortment of mismatched mugs, and questionable decor choices, that have somehow multiplied over the years. The furniture is also getting its moment in the spotlight, as they prepare it for the brave souls, who will attempt to fit everything into a van, that seems to get smaller every time they look at it. Will it all fit in? Will someone accidentally pack that one thing they swear they need? Only time, and possibly a lot of creative stacking and strategic shoving will tell!

By this point, Lorraine and McMatters were running on fumes, exhausted and slightly bewildered by the chaotic whirlwind of boxes, bubble wrap, and the occasional rogue sock, that seemed to have developed a mind of its own. McMatters couldn't help but think back to why he had sworn off moving houses in the past. It was like trying to herd cats, while juggling chainsaws... utterly chaotic with a hint of madness! Meanwhile, Lorraine was practically vibrating with impatience, her excitement for their new home, overshadowed by an overwhelming desire for everything to be finished already. After all, today she had reached her limit; she had officially had enough of moving house! If only they could just snap their fingers, and have all those pesky boxes magically unpacked, because let's face it, who enjoys sorting through endless kitchen utensils, while trying to figure out what half of them even are?

Moving in with McMatters

Upon arriving at McMatters' place, both Jeffery and Susan were waiting with a tray, holding homemade lemonade, a nice refreshing drink, that was well needed. It was as if they had just stepped out of a quaint summer postcard, complete with the sun shining brightly overhead, and birds chirping in harmonious agreement about how delightful this moment was. The lemonade sparkled in the sunlight like liquid sunshine itself, practically begging to be consumed.

"Ah, homemade lemonade! Just what I need after battling rush hour traffic, which is basically like being stuck in a slow-moving conga line led by a particularly stubborn tortoise," McMatters quipped as he gratefully accepted a glass.

Lorraine chimed in with an exaggerated sigh of relief, "I would have traded all my snacks for this citrusy elixir, there's nothing more refreshing than something made from actual lemons, and not some mysterious powder from the back of my cupboard!"

As they took their first sips, it felt as though their taste buds were throwing a party to celebrate surviving the day, complete with confetti made of sugar, and zest! Indeed, nothing quite beats the charm of good company, paired with a deliciously cool drink on an ordinary day, that suddenly became extraordinary.

"Relax a little, guys. Grab a drink," said McMatters to Lorraine's security team. "You earned a rest for a minute."

"Thanks, boss!" Both members of the Alpha team said in unison.

"Bravo Team are on their way. As soon as they arrive, we will get this furniture upstairs. For now, we will put it in the second room on the right, as you get to the top," said McMatters.

McMatters took one look at Lorraine and couldn't help but notice that she seemed more distracted than a cat in a room full of laser pointers. Her usual vibrant complexion, which typically radiated warmth like a sun-kissed olive, had transformed into something resembling the colour of unbuttered toast, pale and slightly alarming. It was as if she had just seen a ghost, or maybe just realized that the coffee machine was broken again. McMatters raised an eyebrow, pondering whether it was something she had eaten, or if perhaps she'd been struck by the sudden existential dread, that often accompanies blood and guts. Either way, he figured it was time to investigate what had knocked the life out of her usual zest!

"Lorraine... are you OK?" asked McMatters.

"I think so, just a little tired. Maybe I just need some food. I will be fine, I'm sure," said Lorraine.

"I will get some tea rustled up for you all. It's hard work moving house; you need to keep your strength up," said Susan.

"Thank you, Susan, that would be fantastic," said McMatters.

When Bravo team finally rolled up to McMatters' place, they were greeted by a sight that could only be described as a picnic gone rogue. There, in the glorious sunshine, everyone was lounging about like they were at a beach resort, rather than engaged in a high-stakes operation. Yes, even Alpha team were present, looking suspiciously relaxed as they munched on sandwiches, and pretended that their mission involved more gourmet dining than tactical manoeuvres. It was the kind of setup, that made you wonder if someone had mistakenly scheduled a barbecue, instead of a serious assignment, because nothing says "elite military operation," quite like people sitting around in folding chairs with plates piled high with food. If there's one thing, we learned that day, it's that teamwork makes the dream work, even if your dream involves potato salad, and questionable jokes about enemy forces being "grilled!"

"Pull up a chair, guys. Plenty of food to go around," said Susan.

"Thank you very much." Team Bravo answered.

For the next half hour, they all basked in the rare delight of being able to take time out of their normal busy schedules, to engage in conversation, an experience so uncommon for any member of the security team, that it felt almost like winning the lottery. It was as if someone had declared a spontaneous holiday from the usual routine of scanning ID badges, and monitoring surveillance feeds. Laughter erupted as they shared tales of their most ridiculous encounters on the job, including one memorable incident involving a rogue squirrel, that had managed to infiltrate a high-security area. Who knew that beneath their serious exteriors, they could be such a rowdy bunch? It was a welcome break from their typical day-to-day grind, where small talk usually revolved around which vending machine snack provided the best energy boost for those late-night shifts.

"Okay, guys, let's get this furniture upstairs, and then things can return to normal," said McMatters.

Lorraine remained quiet, a master of the art of discretion, like a ninja at a karaoke party. She joined in the laughter, chuckling politely as if she were an audience member at a comedy club, but that's as far as Lorraine went. You see, engaging in the delightful chaos of conversation was not her forte; she preferred to observe from the side-lines, silently judging everyone's punchlines, while calculating how long it would take before someone inevitably tripped over their own joke. McMatters was concerned.

Rest

Lorraine couldn't quite put her finger on the source of her sudden sense of unease. A wave of fatigue washed over her, accompanied by a gnawing queasiness that made her stomach churn uncomfortably. It was entirely possible that her physical discomfort stemmed from something as simple as hunger, as she realized with a sinking feeling, that her last meal had been dinner the previous day. In the whirlwind of activity that characterized her life, the constant rush and relentless pace, she had neglected one of life's fundamental necessities: nourishment. The demands of daily responsibilities and the incessant pressure to keep moving forward, had left little room for something as crucial as taking a moment to eat. The feeling didn't shift after eating; in fact, if anything, Lorraine found herself feeling even more drained and fatigued. This overwhelming sense of tiredness could very well be attributed to a food coma, that all-too-familiar sensation that follows a heavy meal, where one's body diverts energy to the digestive process.

However, one must be cautious about dismissing this fatigue as merely a temporary state. Such persistent lethargy might signal underlying issues related to diet, or overall health. Lorraine decided that she urgently needed to sleep, even though it was still quite early, a mere eight o'clock in the evening. However, at that moment, she felt as if she were akin to one of those antiquated computers that would crash unexpectedly, and shut down without warning, a frustrating phenomenon that left users stranded in a sea of unfinished tasks, and lost progress. The weight of exhaustion pressed heavily upon her, clouding her thoughts and dulling her senses. Just like those old machines struggling under the burden of too many processes running simultaneously, Lorraine sensed her own mental faculties faltering, unable to keep pace with the demands of her day-to-day life.

McMatters's

As McMatters stepped into the dimly lit bedroom, a sense of unease washed over him at the sight before him. There lays Lorraine, utterly exhausted and completely unaware of her surroundings, sprawled out on the bed in a most precarious manner. She hadn't quite managed to settle herself properly for the night; instead, she was positioned in a haphazard way. Half on the bed, and half off it, her body awkwardly contorted sideways, as if she were caught in a restless dream. With careful deliberation, McMatters made his way around to the other side of the bed, his heart heavy with concern. The covers were rumpled and dishevelled, a stark contrast to what should have been a peaceful sanctuary for rest. He gently pulled back the sheets to create a cosy nest for her and noticed her shoes. Not carelessly tossed aside on the floor, remnants of an evening that had perhaps spiralled out of control. With the utmost tenderness, he removed Lorraine's shoes, an act that felt both intimate and necessary, as he prepared to lift her into her proper repose. He cradled her with caution, mindful not to jostle or disturb her fragile state, as he carefully placed her into the bed. Tucking her in snugly beneath the warm covers seemed like an essential gesture; it was not just about comfort, but also about safeguarding her from whatever turmoil had led to this chaotic moment. In that hushed space filled with shadows and silence, McMatters felt an overwhelming sense of responsibility, not only for Lorraine's physical comfort, but also for ensuring she would wake up safe and sound when morning light broke through once more.

Lorraine might exhibit considerable strength in various aspects, a realization that McMatters has come to understand through the lessons learned from recent events. However, it is essential to recognize, that despite her resilience, Lorraine possesses vulnerabilities that could be easily overlooked. This duality of strength and frailty serves as a reminder of the complexities inherent in human nature. Consequently, McMatters feels a profound sense of responsibility to protect her as much as possible, aware that while she may appear formidable on the surface, there are deeper insecurities and challenges lurking beneath the surface. His protective actions are not merely instinctual; they stem from a recognition of her fragility in certain circumstances, prompting him to act as a shield against potential harm and adversity.

Chapter Thirty-Four

The Book Shop

The Slaters were now in a state of desperation that could rival a soap opera cliffhanger. Their fearless leader, Anthony, affectionately dubbed Tony by his loyal followers, likely as a nod to the fact that he wasn't getting a raise anytime soon, found himself precariously perched on the edge of chaos, with only nine men at his side with himself making up the tenth. Yes, folks, it was a real party of ten, or perhaps more accurately described as a party gone horribly wrong. The group had run out of real food two days ago, leaving them to grapple with their dwindling supplies like starving wolves circling a particularly stubborn deer that just wouldn't give in. And just when you thought things couldn't get worse, they were now confronted with the alarming reality of having no water either.

Yes, the essential life-sustaining liquid, that humans have been relying on since time immemorial. It was as if they had entered some twisted reality show, where survival meant sacrificing sanity along with their last crumbs of granola. As time dragged on like molasses in January, tension within their makeshift camp inside the bookstore escalated to levels, that would make even seasoned referee's flinch. The smokers among them were beginning to climb the walls, from intense cravings a sight that might have been amusing under different circumstances but was now akin to watching caged animals pacing back and forth in agitation. Their bodies and minds had become more restless than cats at bath time, as withdrawal symptoms set in like uninvited guests who showed up hours late to the party. The lack of cigarettes was exacerbating an already stressful situation; inner arguments erupted among the men, like sudden storms on an otherwise calm sea, one minute there's peace and quiet; then bam! Out come the emotional lightning bolts! Each confrontation added fuel to an already volatile atmosphere filled with anxiety and frustration. They weren't just struggling against their physical needs; oh no! They were also grappling with each other's rising tempers and fears, as if they were contestants in some bizarre game show titled "Who Can Drive Their Friends Crazy First?"

Slater realized with a surge of urgency, akin to a cat that has just spotted the dreaded vacuum cleaner, that they could no longer linger in the bookstore. The atmosphere was so thick with tension one could practically slice it with a butter knife, not that anyone would want to attempt such a feat. He could feel the weight of their predicament pressing down on him like an overstuffed backpack, filled with textbooks and bad decisions. Once they stepped outside, he knew it would be like diving headfirst into a swimming pool of uncertainty, where the water might just be shark infested. The events surrounding the Blythes were looming in his mind like an unwanted family reunion; their reckless antics had transformed them from innocent bookworms into prime targets for revenge seekers, who undoubtedly had less-than-pleasant intentions. With this sobering realization and perhaps a touch of panic that felt akin to realizing his favourite snack was all gone, Tony understood there was an urgent need for a well-thought-out plan to navigate the perilous path ahead, without tripping over their own shoelaces. It wasn't merely about finding a cosy corner to huddle in safety. This was about ensuring they didn't become unwitting participants in some sort of twisted game of cat and mouse, where they were decidedly more mouse than cat. He needed to concoct an ingenious strategy, one that would keep them one step ahead of anyone who might come after them, think Mission Impossible but without Tom Cruise and way more awkwardness. Relying on his quick thinking, resourcefulness, and perhaps an inexplicable ability to find snacks under pressure, he aimed to outmanoeuvre any lurking dangers, as if he were playing chess against someone who only knew how to move pawns.

"Grant. We can't stay here any longer. If I take three-quarters of the team, could you and the others run a mission—let's call it a backup plan in case things go wrong?"

"Yes, sure, what are your thoughts?"

"Well, when we blew up Blythe's car, you said a woman came out of Blythe's house."

"Oh yes, I figured she was somehow part of the family."

"As an insurance plan, could you grab her and hold her? I want to make sure we have a backup plan we can work with."

"Consider it done."

Slater felt an immense sense of relief wash over him, like a warm blanket on a chilly winter night, knowing that he had something to back them up. This was not merely a precaution; it was an essential resource they would undoubtedly require, if they were to successfully navigate their way out of the bookshop in one piece, preferably with their sanity intact. The atmosphere within the shop was thick with tension, so dense it could probably be sliced with a butter knife. Shadows loomed ominously, cast by the towering shelves filled with dusty tomes, that seemed to whisper secrets as they passed by. Each creak of the wooden floorboards beneath their feet sounded like an ominous warning bell, echoing through the eerie silence and reminding Slater what challenges lay ahead.

He could almost hear the books chuckling at their predicament, as if they were all in on some cosmic joke, while he and his crew were left in suspense about how this plot twist would unfold. Without this backup plan, a collection of obscure spells or perhaps just some good snacks, their chances of overcoming whatever ridiculous obstacles awaited them would be significantly diminished. Armed not only with determination, but also with an overwhelming desire to avoid becoming permanent residents among the forgotten volumes, they braced themselves for what lay beyond those heavy, book-laden walls which probably housed more mysteries than answers, and enough dust bunnies to fill a small vacuum cleaner.

Santos

Santos was standing there minding his own business, being older he blends into the background better, when he caught sight of a group of about nine or ten men spilling out from the back entrance of the bookstore. Now, let me tell you, these guys looked like they were up to no good, and had a plan. Talk about an unsettling sight! It was as if they were auditioning for a role in a low-budget thriller where the plot twist involved something decidedly unsavoury, all ducking and diving. Feeling his internal alarm bells ringing louder than a fire truck at rush hour, Santos felt an overwhelming sense of urgency wash over him. This wasn't just any ordinary group of dudes; this was potentially the beginning of some serious shenanigans! With adrenaline pumping through his veins, and visions of heroism dancing in his head (or perhaps just visions of running away), he lunged for his phone like it was about to sprout wings and fly off.

He quickly punched in Jarvis's number. This wasn't your average chit-chat call to discuss last night's game or share a particularly funny cat video. No, this was more like an urgent bat signal sent through the digital ether. It screamed that something suspicious was brewing, and time was not on their side! Every second felt precious as he relayed what could only be described as the literary equivalent of impending doom. Safety first, laughter second, but let's be honest: if things went sideways, there might not be time for either! Santos was worried about what was coming next.

"Hi Jarvis, it's Santos. Listen, a group of men just left the book shop, looks like they are on the move."

"Okay, it's about time too. I will phone Bennett now."

Santos kept watching and waiting, his unease growing with each passing moment. The scene unfolded before him as the group of individuals suddenly split into three distinct groups, each climbing into separate vehicles, three cars in total. This unexpected decision puzzled Santos deeply; after all, they could have easily fit their numbers into just two cars without any issue. The presence of a third vehicle raised a host of alarming questions in his mind. Was it a precautionary measure, perhaps indicating that they anticipated trouble? Or was it possible that they were just trying to confuse anyone who might be monitoring their movements? As he pondered these possibilities, a sense of foreboding washed over him, urging him to remain vigilant and cautious about what might happen next.

Jarvis

"Hi Bennett, we are gone. The Slaters are on the move at the back of the bookshop." Jarvis said.

"Okay, I'm on my way. I will tell you more once I know something."

After Jarvis hung up the phone, he immediately dialled his team members, eager to relay the information he had just received.

"Hi guys. Okay, we have movement at the back of the book shop, can you guys keep tabs on Blythe as well? I don't want him ruining our chance to get hold of the leader, because he wants revenge."

"Will do, boss."

Once he had finished coordinating with his team, it was time to inform Blythe about what was unfolding. The urgency of the situation weighed on him; time was of the essence, and every second counted at this critical moment.

"Blythe, the Slaters have started moving out of the bookshop. Remember what I said—do not do a thing. I have a plan."

"Okay."

Jarvis still didn't trust Blythe as far as he could throw him, reflecting a deep-seated scepticism, that stems from past experiences and interactions. This phrase encapsulates a fundamental mistrust, suggesting that Jarvis perceives Blythe as unreliable or deceitful. The expression itself implies that the level of trust is so minimal, that it would be virtually impossible for Jarvis to consider any close association, or collaboration with Blythe without feeling uneasy. Such sentiments can often arise in professional environments where individuals have encountered dishonesty or betrayal, leading to caution and wariness in future dealings. This lingering doubt underscores the complexities of human relationships, particularly when trust has been compromised. It also serves as a reminder of how previous actions can heavily influence current perceptions, and future interactions.

Bennetts

Bennett was watching and waiting as the three cars moved towards the main road. He noticed that two cars, one with Slater in it went one way, and the other car went another. this he found curious.

"Santos, are you seeing this?"

"Yes, I will take the single car so you can follow the other two. You never know, they might split again."

"Good idea. Talk later."

Bennett found himself lost in contemplation, pondering whether the Slaters would resort to their previous tactic of dividing the cars once more. This strategy could potentially complicate any efforts to track down Slater himself, creating a web of uncertainty and confusion for anyone trying to keep tabs on him. The thought nagged at him; after all, the Slaters were known for their cunning and resourcefulness. Splitting up the vehicles would not only obscure their movements but would also serve as a clever ploy to throw off anyone who might be tailing them. This intricate game of cat and mouse, intensified Bennett's curiosity and concern, leaving him to consider just how far they would go to maintain their elusive advantage.

Blythe

Blythe was consumed by a burning desire for revenge against the Slaters, a vendetta that had been ignited by a series of unforgivable transgressions. First, they brazenly stole a crucial shipment, an act that not only stripped him of valuable goods, but also dealt a severe blow to his reputation in the underworld. Then, as if that betrayal wasn't enough, they went on to seriously injure two of his trusted men. Loyal associates who relied on him for their livelihoods. This reckless violence not only harmed those close to him, but also severely impacted his income and financial stability. To add insult to injury, they even had the audacity to blow up his own car, leaving nothing but twisted metal in their wake.

Oh yes, Blythe wants revenge alright. His fury is palpable and growing with each passing moment, as he plots how best to make the Slaters pay for their treachery, in ways they could never have anticipated. But Jarvis and Lorraine had both emphatically stated that he couldn't take any action until they successfully captured Slater, making it a critical priority for the group. It was clear that everyone needed to be present at that crucial moment, as their collective efforts would determine the outcome of their plans. The tension in the air was palpable; time was of the essence, and with every passing second, the stakes grew higher. Without Slater in their grasp, and the full team assembled, any attempt to move forward would be futile and could jeopardize everything they were working toward. Blythe's eyes were fixed intently on the car that sped away, its tires screeching in protest the tarmac. With a surge of adrenaline coursing through his veins, he disregarded everything else, the other vehicle that veered off into an uncharted path, now fading into the distance. His focus was razor-sharp; he could not afford to let this opportunity slip away. Every second counted as he pursued a lead that could unravel everything that he had been chasing for many weeks.

Slater

The Slaters had begun to distance themselves from the quaint little bookshop, a deliberate move that underscored their growing apprehension. As they reached the traffic lights, they abruptly turned right. Meanwhile, the other two vehicles, including the one in which Slater himself was traveling in, continued straight along the road leading out of town. A sudden uncertainty gnawed at him. He pondered how many individuals were pursuing him, or perhaps even trailing behind the other team involved in this precarious mission. In that moment of doubt and tension, Slater couldn't shake off his hope that every member of their group was adhering to his carefully crafted plan. The operation hinged, not only on his ability to remain undetected, but also on a coordinated effort to successfully abduct the woman who was pivotal to their objectives. He understood all too well, that any misstep could have dire consequences. Not just for him and his team, but potentially for everything they had meticulously orchestrated up until now. The stakes were high, and as he pressed forward into uncertain territory, he felt an acute awareness of both fear and resolve coursing through him.

Slater had personal stakes that were deeply entwined with his ambitions in this perilous game. He led a small, tight-knit team, forged not just by shared goals, but also by the bonds of camaraderie that resembled those of a family. Over the years, they had endured unimaginable losses, watching many friends and allies perish in their relentless pursuit of success, and survival within this brutal world. Each death was a stark reminder of the high cost associated with their endeavours, and served to further solidify their resolve. As Slater reflected on their harrowing journey, he recognized that they were tantalizingly close to achieving something monumental.

Just a little longer and he knew he could leverage his hard-fought position to forcefully carve out a seat at the proverbial table, alongside some of the most formidable names in the underworld. This opportunity was not merely about power or recognition; it represented validation for all they had sacrificed along the way, making every loss feel even heavier considering what was at stake.

Slater and his team embarked on a journey to a dilapidated building, that had long been left to the ravages of time. An abandoned mansion, that stood as a haunting reminder of its former grandeur. Overgrown vines crept up its weathered façade, and shattered windows whispered tales of neglect and decay. This small mansion, once a symbol of elegance, had fallen into disrepair after years of abandonment. However, Slater saw potential where others only saw ruin. He took it upon himself to reclaim this forgotten structure, pouring his efforts into restoring it. Not just as a project, but as a personal sanctuary, a place where he could impose his vision, and breathe new life into the walls that had absorbed so many stories over the years. The question remains: was Slater's restoration an act of redemption for the house, or merely an exercise in self-indulgence?

Jarvis

Jarvis arrived just in the nick of time, his eyes widening as he witnessed the split between the two cars, like a dramatic scene straight out of an action movie. Blythe, with all the grace of a cat on roller skates, chased after the two vehicles with fervour, his intent on revenge now very clear, while Bennett followed close behind watching both the Slaters and Blythe. Meanwhile, Santos had his sights set on the other car. Let's not forget Jarvis's team! They were right behind Santos, who was puzzled at the split, trying to figure out if they were in an elaborate game of follow-the-leader, to reduce the amount who followed the Slaters, or if they were up to something else. But one thing was for sure: this was going to be one wild ride! Jarvis arriving just as the cars split, decided he'd follow the two cars, he felt he might need to restrain Blythe.

They all pulled up outside the grand entrance of a mansion, that looked like it had been lifted straight from a movie about wealthy eccentrics complete with gargoyles, that seemed to be judging their very existence, and fountains that gushed water as if they were auditioning for a role in "The Greatest Showman." As they stepped out of their vehicles, which were less "luxury cars" and more "what on earth are we doing here?" A peculiar assortment of rust buckets, quirky hatchbacks, and one car that might have been on loan from a 90s sitcom, they gathered in a huddle like kids before a big game, whispering strategies and exchanging nervous glances.

It was as if they were preparing to face not just the mansion, but whatever bizarre adventures awaited them inside. One could almost hear the dramatic music swell in the background as they stood there, hearts racing at what lay beyond those ornate doors.

"Alright, team," said Jarvis.

"How do you want to play this?" asked Bennett.

"Let's follow the same process as the farmhouse, but this time I want them alive, bound, gagged, and taken to a different location."

"Where are you thinking?"

"The old shopping mall. It hasn't been in use for seven years, so it's the perfect place."

"I will take two," said Bennett.

"I will take Slater," said Blythe.

"No, Blythe. I promise I will let you play once we are there, but I will take Slater. You know why."

"Let's move, guys." said Jarvis.

They crept towards the mansion staying out of sight.

Chapter Thirty-Five

The Police Station

Detective Winters had not enjoyed a single win on any case since stepping into the shoes of Detective Jackson. However, as promising as her start had been, the reality was weighing heavily. Each day that passed without resolution added weight to her shoulders, and she could feel the pressure mounting, like an impending storm cloud. With every unanswered question and every lead that faded into nothingness, her confidence wavered. The expectations from her superiors loomed large, and whispers among colleagues hinted at doubt regarding her capabilities. As she walked through the bustling precinct, filled with seasoned detectives who had solved countless cases, she couldn't shake off the nagging feeling that time was running out for her to prove herself in this demanding line of work.

"OK, let's gather around." She spoke, with her team now huddled together, Detective Winters hoped for some good news.

"Does anyone have anything on the Detective Jackson case?" Everyone looked around with blank expressions.

"What about the two bodies in the street?" Her voice now sounded desperate, but still, no one had any information to share.
"The pub, anything about who committed the bloodbath?" Dread set in. "And has anything come back from the lab about the house of blood with no bodies?"

All her team were silent, a thick tension hanging in the air, like an unwelcome fog. No one dared to break the stillness; they were all paralyzed by uncertainty and fear. With no leads to follow and not a single person willing to speak up. The chilling reality of their situation gnawed at Detective Winters, sending shivers down her spine. Who on earth wielded such immense power, that even the most hardened criminals would think twice before whispering a name? The city, sprawling and vibrant, typically buzzed with the activities of various local factions, that operated in its shadows like small cogs in a much larger machine, but today it felt different. Normally, amidst the chaos of street dealings and backroom negotiations, there would always be someone willing to betray their own for a price, or perhaps out of sheer desperation.

Yet now, an unsettling hush blanketed these once-boisterous corners; this time, something far more sinister lurked beneath the surface. Detective Winters could feel it deep within her bones. This was not just another case of gang warfare or turf battles. This was something altogether darker and more insidious. All those small groups she had relied on for information, were now hiding in fear, their bravado stripped away as they sensed that they were playing against forces beyond their control. Winter's instincts screamed at her that this was indeed a dark day, a day where shadows loomed larger than ever before, and she knew they needed to tread carefully, if they hoped to uncover the truth lurking just out of reach.

Chapter Thirty-Six

Lorraine

Lorraine was at McMatters trying to sort out her things. As she tried to figure out the best place to stash her belongings, she suddenly spotted Susan making her way upstairs. A sense of hope washed over her; maybe Susan would have some clever ideas or solutions for organizing her stuff. After all, Susan always seemed to have a knack for finding creative ways to make space and keep things tidy!

"Hi Susan, do you have a minute?"

"Yes, of course. What can I help you with?"

Lorraine gestured to all her things with her arm. "I'm not sure where to put them all."

"Oh, we can sort that out, no problem."

Susan strolled over to what Lorraine initially believed was just a plain wall. With a curious touch, she pressed on five different panels, each one revealing something incredible. The first panel swung open to unveil a spacious walk-in wardrobe, bathed in soft overhead lighting that made everything inside sparkle. It was like stepping into a fashion dream! The next panel revealed cleverly designed drawers at the bottom, perfect for storing all sorts of items. Then came the third panel, which opened to showcase a stunning vanity table, that seemed straight out of a Hollywood movie; it had elegant mirrors and just the right amount of charm for getting ready before a big night out. They revealed his clothes neatly hung or folded, everything organized with an impressive level of care. It was clear that this space wasn't just functional; it had been thoughtfully arranged, reflecting both Susan's flair and Steve's personality! Susan then touched a side panel that held almost all of Steve's shoes. She gestured at the right-hand side panel, and Lorraine walked over and touched it. Out popped a space for her shoes, and Lorraine loved it!

"All around the room is hidden storage; it keeps things tidy and elegant."

"Thank you, Susan, for your help."

"You're welcome, Lorraine."

Lorraine was in the middle of unpacking her belongings, surrounded by a mountain of boxes, that seemed to multiply by the minute, as if they were auditioning for a role in a horror movie titled "The Boxes That Ate My Living Room." She took a moment to survey her new space, excitement bubbling up within her like freshly brewed coffee at dawn, as she envisioned how it would all come together. Pictures hung perfectly on the walls, stylish furniture arranged just so, and perhaps even an artisanal cheese platter laid out, for any unsuspecting guests who dared to visit. Just as she was halfway through organizing her stuff, trying with all her might to channel her inner Marie Kondo, while fighting off a mountain of bubble wrap and old pizza boxes from last week's move-in party, her phone buzzed unexpectedly with a call. She glanced at the screen and saw it was Jarvis, Lorraine answered the call, bracing herself for whatever ridiculousness he had in store this time.

Jarvis

Jarvis firmly resolved that it was imperative to ensure Lorraine and McMatters reached their destination before anyone else. Recognizing the importance of their timely arrival, he understood that every moment counted. The stakes were high, and he was determined to navigate any obstacles in their path with precision and efficiency. With a clear plan in mind, Jarvis set into motion the necessary steps to secure their advantage, fully aware that this strategic move could alter the course of events for everyone involved.

"Hi Lorraine, it's time. Can you get Steve and make your way to the derelict shopping mall?" Asked Jarvis

"Yes, okay we will see you there." Replied Lorraine.

The Old Shopping Mall

Lorraine and McMatters arrived promptly at the old shopping mall, their excitement palpable as they stepped through the worn glass doors, instantly transported back to a time when this bustling hub was alive with activity. With wide eyes and eager hearts, they began searching for just the right spot to set up for the much-anticipated event with the Slaters. The atmosphere was charged with possibility, each corner of the mall whispering tales of its vibrant past.

McMatters, ever prepared for adventure, had brought along a sturdy duffel bag, that slung comfortably over his shoulder. Its contents were a mystery waiting to be unveiled. Meanwhile, Lorraine clutched her newly acquired knife tightly, a gleaming tool not only meant for practical purposes, but also a symbol of her readiness to embrace whatever challenges lay ahead. The blade sparkled under the fluorescent lights, hinting at thrilling possibilities and new experiences, that awaited them in this intriguing location. Together, they were on the brink of an exhilarating journey!

"Lorraine, can you help me set up the area please?"
McMatters asked. "We need seating for each family, a
place for them to put any weapons they might have, and
enough space in the middle for Slater to be placed."

"Yes, no problem."

They eagerly set about preparing the area, moving in
perfect harmony and synchronicity, as if they were
dancers performing an intricate choreography. Each
person instinctively understood what the other needed at
any given moment, anticipating their actions with
remarkable precision. It was a beautiful display of
teamwork, where every glance and gesture
communicated unspoken intentions. The air was filled
with an electric energy as they collaborated seamlessly,
transforming the space into something truly special with
their collective efforts.

Once all was set up, they waited in silence, their hearts
racing with anticipation as they prepared themselves for
the exhilarating road ahead. The air was thick with
excitement, filled with the electric energy of possibilities
that lay before them. Each moment felt charged, as if
time itself was holding its breath in awe of what was to
come. They exchanged knowing glances, each one
reflecting a mix of determination and eagerness, ready to
embrace whatever challenges or adventures awaited
them on this journey. The horizon beckoned like a
shimmering promise, inviting them to step forward into
the unknown and discover what lay beyond their current
reality. Lorraine's formidable bodyguards stood like
silent sentinels at the entrance to the bustling shopping
mall, their impressive figures creating a protective
barrier, that granted Lorraine and McMatters a rare
moment of privacy, amidst the chaotic energy running
through their veins. Lorraine walked over to McMatters
and embraced him and gave him a loving kiss while they
killed time.

Jarvis

Jarvis took charge with unwavering authority, commanding everyone to converge on the mansion with a sense of urgency and purpose. As they stormed through the door, adrenaline coursing through their veins, the Slaters sprang into action, fiercely retaliating against the intruders. Bullets whizzed through the air like deadly wasps, ricocheting off walls, and creating a cacophony of chaos, that echoed throughout the cavernous space. Each shot fired was a testament to their desperation and determination to defend their territory at all costs. In this high-stakes confrontation, every second counted as tension mounted and danger lurked in every shadow.

With a deafening silence enveloping the mansion, a palpable tension filled the air, and just like that, the hunt began in earnest. Room by room, they methodically searched for Slater, driven by an unwavering determination. Shadows loomed in every corner, as they moved through the grand hallways adorned with opulent chandeliers, that now seemed to dim under the weight of their mission. The creak of floorboards echoed ominously beneath their feet, each sound amplifying their sense of urgency and resolve.

At the end of the upstairs corridor stood the last room, that had yet to be checked, and Jarvis firmly indicated for everyone to move aside from the walls, as he prepared to open the door. With a swift motion, he flung the door open and instinctively ducked down, signalling his team to follow him into the uncertain darkness of the room. One by one, they entered cautiously, their hearts pounding with anticipation. It was there that they found Slater, the last man standing in this tense standoff, huddled alone in a corner. He sat there trembling uncontrollably from sheer fear, his body wracked with panic as tears streamed down his face like rivulets of

despair. The sight was haunting. It underscored not only his isolation in that moment, but also the profound impact of their harrowing situation. But a strange thing happened: Slater began to laugh uncontrollably.
The laughter erupted from him like a sudden storm, growing louder and more boisterous with each passing moment. It was as if he had been struck by a wave of infectious joy, his mirth resonating through the air, like the jubilant calls of a wild hog in the throes of delight. The sound was both unexpected and captivating, drawing attention from all around, as his laughter filled the space with an undeniable energy that could not be contained. His laughter had a sinister tone, though Jarvis had a bad feeling that Slater had a backup plan.

"Tie him up, gag him, and carry him downstairs." said Jarvis.

The Bennetts executed this action decisively, fully aware of their objective, while Jarvis took charge of retrieving the car and manoeuvring it closer to the front door. This coordinated effort underscored their sense of urgency and determination, as they worked seamlessly together to ensure that everything fell into place perfectly. The leader of the Bennetts noticed Blythe's face.

"Don't even think about it. I will not hesitate to stop you, Blythe."

Blythe was seething, a tempest of fury boiling up inside him, as he struggled to maintain control over his body. Every fibre of his being was consumed by a burning desire for revenge, a craving so intense that it felt almost palpable. The fiery anger coursed through his veins, urging him to act, to unleash the pent-up rage that threatened to erupt at any moment. It was as if he were a volcano on the brink of an explosive eruption, desperately trying to contain the molten fury within, while plotting how best to exact his retribution. The

217

thought of vengeance overshadowed all rationality, driving him deeper into a frenzy, as he envisioned the moment when he would finally claim what he believed was rightfully his.

"Meet you all at the derelict shopping mall," said Jarvis, as Slater was placed in his boot.

While driving to the mall, Jarvis phoned Santos. Santos had cautiously followed the other car, accompanied by a team of Jarvis's men. The other car sped through the dimly lit streets. Each bump in the road made his heart race faster, a mixture of adrenaline and dread coursing through his veins. He couldn't shake off the feeling of impending danger; every sharp turn taken by the car ahead felt like a step deeper into uncertainty. What were they up to? Where were they going? The weight of these questions hung heavily in the air, as he strained to keep his eyes fixed on their target, hoping against hope that he wouldn't lose them in this labyrinthine chase. After an hour had passed, a growing sense of unease began to settle over Santos. With increasing apprehension, he decided it would be prudent to drop back a little and allow Jarvis's team to take the lead. He felt that a change of cars might be necessary, considering the uncertain circumstances they were facing. However, thirty minutes later, as they continued driving through what seemed like an endless stretch of road, dread crept into his mind. Santos couldn't shake the feeling that they were going around in circles, a grim realization that left him increasingly anxious about their situation. The horizon appeared unchanged, and with each passing moment, he became more acutely aware of their dwindling fuel supply. The nagging worry that they might soon run out of petrol loomed larger in his thoughts, like a dark cloud overhead. In a moment of urgency mixed with concern for his team's safety, he picked up his phone and dialled Jarvis's team, hoping for answers or perhaps even reassurance, amid the uncertainty enveloping them.

"Guys, I have a feeling they will run our tanks dry, and then carry out their plan. I will pull off for more fuel and then catch back up with you," said Santos.

"Good idea. We can switch after, and we will do the same."

After Santos had filled up with fuel, Jarvis phoned. It was just as Santos was re-joining his team.

"Jarvis! How's it going?"

"We have Slater. I'm on my way to the old derelict shopping mall. What's happening on your end?"

"We are driving non-stop, sometimes in circles. I felt they were trying to drain our fuel before carrying out something, God knows what, but I have a bad feeling."

"Do you have enough fuel?"

"We do now. I stopped a few minutes ago and filled up. Your guys are currently filling up. We took turns."

"Very good, Santos. I have a bad feeling too."

"You will need to deal with Slater. I won't get there at this rate."

"Not a problem, Santos. Whereabouts in town, are you?"

"West, currently. It's like we are sticking close to one area. I'm not sure yet what these idiots are up to, though."

"Okay, ring me later."

Chapter Thirty-Seven

The Mall

Jarvis, the Bennetts, and the Blythe's all converged on the derelict shopping mall. It had seen better days, like way better. It was so run down that even the pigeons looked like they were thinking about relocating. As Jarvis scanned the scene, his keen eyes landed on Lorraine's bodyguards, who looked like they had just stepped off a movie set about tough guys playing tough guys. They directed Jarvis with all the grace of a bouncer at an exclusive club, pointing out where McMatters and Lorraine were holed up amidst the crumbling walls. With a nod that said both "I approve" and "This is definitely not what I expected," Jarvis surveyed their chosen hideout within the mall, a clothing department store for a big brand, three stories high. They were located on the third floor of the four-storey mall.

"Tie Slater to the chair," directed Jarvis.

"You all know the score: weapons on the tables, one table per family. Get comfy," said McMatters.

Lorraine had never encountered a setup quite like this before, so she stood by, eyes wide and mouth slightly agape, like a kid at a candy store who has just spotted the giant gumball machine. With her arms crossed and an exaggerated expression of curiosity plastered on her face, she watched intently, ready to spring into action the moment it was her turn. You could practically see the gears turning in her head, as she mentally prepared herself for whatever zany adventure awaited. Lorraine was all in; after all, nothing says "fun" quite like waiting quietly in suspense. Once everyone was seated, Blythe stood up, his face twisted with anger. You could almost see the steam coming out of his ears, His glare could've melted steel, and if looks could kill.

"Sit down Blythe, I will not repeat it again!" Jarvis said in a tone that sent shivers down your spine, Blythe sat down.

Jarvis, McMatters, and Lorraine huddled together like a trio of secret agents preparing for a top-secret mission, complete with hushed whispers and exaggerated hand gestures. After a few minutes of intense strategic planning, that felt more like an episode of a sitcom than actual scheming, they finally reached a consensus: Lorraine would take on the role of the middleman, essentially the human equivalent of the filling in a well-stacked club sandwich. Meanwhile, McMatters would oversee torture, which he took far too seriously. And then there was Jarvis, who would steal the show like an overly dramatic actor craving applause at every turn. With Lorraine's negotiation skills on board, and hopefully lots of torture involved, it seemed they had devised quite the plan.

McMatters was being sneaky, and he crept around in silence. His stealthy moves rivalling those of a ninja on a sugar high. With the utmost care, he snagged a bowl and placed it under Slater's unsuspecting feet, The water swirled around his feet. Next, McMatters reached into his bag like a magician pulling rabbits out of a hat. He tiptoed over to the nearby socket and plugged the device. Once everything was connected, he turned them all on, and watched intently as sparks flew like fireworks on New Year's Eve! It was just what he needed, a little zap to get things rolling. Slater's eyes went wide, with the fear of what was to come. McMatters decided it was time to shed his jacket, like an overly dramatic actor exiting stage left. He folded it with such elegance, you'd think he was preparing for some kind of fashion show rather than an electrifying experiment. With his sleeves rolled up halfway, he was ready.

"Please turn off the plug?" asked McMatters. Jarvis, now the bystander, switched off the plug.

McMatters placed the wires in the bowl of water. The room was so quiet you could hear a pin drop. That is, until Slater started laughing again.

"What's so funny, Slater?" asked McMatters.

"F. you, but you will regret this, and you will have to live with what my guys are doing."

McMatters dramatically gestured as if he were conducting an orchestra, flicking his finger with flair to activate the switch. Suddenly, zzzzzzzzzzt! A cacophony of electric volts surged through Slater's body, transforming him into a human lightning rod. His hair stood on end like a startled Porcupine, and his eyes bulged out wide in complete shock. He looked like he had just seen his ex at a family reunion! Just as quickly as it had begun, McMatters flicked his finger again with the finesse of a magician performing a trick, and the electrical chaos came to an abrupt halt. Slater flopped back into his chair, resembling a rag doll that had just experienced its first roller coaster ride.

As Slater desperately attempted to regain his composure, tears streamed down his cheeks like a leaky faucet. He continued to laugh so hard, that he could have qualified for an Olympic event in hysterics. Just then, Lorraine strolled over walking slowly and with purpose. The room collectively gasped, as if they had witnessed something unexpected. This startled McMatters, who was filled with unexpected pride. He couldn't help but feel a swell of satisfaction, knowing that Lorraine had reached such formidable heights in her reputation. She instilled genuine fear in everyone around her, like a lioness strutting through the Savannah, while Gazelles nervously glanced over their shoulders. Lorraine crouched down to his level, making her look bigger than she was. With the finesse of a magician, she reached into her pocket and pulled out a tissue. Gently, she dabbed at Slater's tear-streaked face, as if attempting to erase the evidence of his emotional meltdown.

"There, there Slater," she cooed in a soft voice. "Don't cry; I'm sure we can work something out."

With that comforting tone, you'd think she was negotiating peace treaties instead of just trying to salvage whatever dignity Slater had left amidst his waterfall of tears.

"You'll end up like that other woman, when my guys get hold of you," said Slater.

McMatters flicked his finger and once again zzzzzzzzzz, as Slater was zapped. McMatters flicked again, and it stopped.

"I'm sorry Slater. I don't know of any other women, unless you are referring to yourself," said Lorraine.

Slater was seething, a veritable volcano of rage ready to erupt at any moment. He snarled and snapped like a particularly disgruntled bear who just discovered someone had stolen his honey, launching a flurry of insults and name-calling, that flew out of his mouth with the force of a fire-breathing dragon. It was as if he were channelling all the pent-up frustration, of an entire season's worth of reality TV drama, spewing verbal grenades left and right, like a rabid dog on the loose in a small-town park. Just when he thought he had reached peak fury, zzzzzzzzzzt! Out of nowhere, McMatters zapped him yet again, with that infuriatingly smug little gadget of his, a device, that seemed to have been designed specifically for the purpose of turning Slater's raging tirade into nothing more than an amusing spectacle for everyone else in the room.

"Now Slater, care to tell me about this woman? Because I don't know many people you see, so you must ask yourself if I care about someone I don't know," said Lorraine as she wiped Slater's eyes.

"He knows her. It's his fault," Slater looked at Blythe.

"So, you're telling me that Blythe knows this woman?" asked Lorraine.

"Are you stupid? You must be stupid. She lives with him." said Slater.

McMatters glanced nervously at Jarvis, then shot a bemused look at Lorraine, as if trying to decode the situation like it was a particularly confusing crossword puzzle. They all turned their attention to Blythe, who appeared paler than a bowl of vanilla ice cream on a winter's day. It was evident that some realization had hit him like a freight train: Slater had either inflicted harm upon his sister, or in an even more sinister turn of events, had taken her away entirely. The air crackled with tension.

Lorraine

McMatters nodded to Lorraine with an expression that clearly said, "Do you have this under control?" Lorraine responded with a confident nod of her own, which was essentially the equivalent of a superhero giving the green light to sidekick, this was their cue that it was time to unleash her inner chaos. Strutting over to her table with confidence, Lorraine approached the solitary knife resting there. The infamous Bennett's former knife, which had seen better days. With a flourish that would make any magician jealous, she grabbed the knife and began twirling it in the air, like she was auditioning for a role in an action movie. The blade glimmered in the light, as if trying to steal the spotlight from Lorraine herself.

"Remove him from the chair, and the bowl of water, and stand him tied up!" demanded Lorraine.

Jarvis dramatically gestured to McMatters, waving his hand. "Hold it right there! Stay right where you are!" he instructed.

"Don't worry," Jarvis added with a wink, "Lorraine has this under control."

The Bennetts stood up like a bunch of obedient little soldiers, ready to march into whatever chaos Lorraine had cooked up for them, no questions asked. It was as if they had all collectively agreed that questioning Lorraine's leadership, was akin to questioning the laws of gravity, futile and possibly dangerous. Meanwhile, poor Blythe remained seated, looking like a deer caught in the headlights, his face a mix of confusion and worry, so intense it could have powered a small city. He was deeply contemplating the precarious situation. Blythe knew that if he were up there instead of Lorraine, Slater would already be dead, and he would never learn about his sister's fate. Saving her was his top priority. So, there he sat, biting his tongue harder than a child trying not to scream after stepping on a Lego piece in the dark. He desperately hoped that Lorraine had her act together and would manage to gather crucial intel about Blythe's missing sister, before time ran out.

Lorraine circled Slater, her mind racing. Trying to decide upon her next move. She leaned in and whispered urgently to the Bennetts' leader. Without a moment's hesitation, Bennett signalled two others. They sprang into action, swiftly tying a separate rope around Slater's ankles and securing them tightly to the two posts. They stayed at their positions, tense and alert, bracing for what would happen next. Lorraine continued to circle Slater. "Alright, Slater, I will ask you some questions. How you respond will determine your outcome. Do you understand?"

"F. you."

Lorraine approached him with a determined stride and, in one swift motion, slashed down one side of his face. Slater's scream echoed through the room. Unfazed, Lorraine circled him once more and, upon reaching the other side, she demanded with fierce intensity.

"What have you done to Blythe's sister?"

Slater responded with a mocking laugh. "You'll never find out," he taunted.

Without hesitation, Lorraine cut down the other side of his face, eliciting another agonized scream from Slater. This was her way of showing she meant business. She would stop at nothing to uncover the truth.

"Now Slater, so far I have been nice, which these other people will agree." Lorraine turned to the families, who all nodded.

McMatters looked at Jarvis, lost for words. Lorraine walked to the back of Slater. "Where is she, or where do you plan to take her?"

Slater laughed hard, blood trickling down his face. Lorraine grabbed his hair, pulling him down. Ready to drag him closer to the nearby lift.

"Pick him up; he needs to see this next bit," she demanded.

As the Bennetts were busy with the rope, Jarvis stood him up and turned him to face the lift, clearly thinking Lorraine would terrify him.

"Blythe, open these doors, please?" She instructed.

Slater waited anxiously, as Blythe stood there and forced open the doors to the lift, with the help of Jarvis and McMatters.

The Bennetts exchanged anxious glances, uncertain if this was merely a scare tactic by Lorraine, or if she truly intended to put him down the hole. Their worry was palpable, as they caught McMatters' eye. He also seemed to be questioning whether Lorraine would go through with it. With trembling hands, the Bennetts tied the rope around the post just once and clung tightly to its end, their fear evident in every movement.

"Should we try that again, Slater?"

"The bitch is dead, and so will you too," said Slater.

Lorraine moved with an almost magical grace, circling behind Slater before pivoting to face the families. In a breathtakingly swift motion, she side-kicked him. Slater was propelled forward, his screams of "no, no wait no ahhhhh" echoing through the air as he plummeted halfway down the shaft. McMatters and Jarvis were left gasping in sheer disbelief. They never imagined she would leap straight into such dramatic action, kicking him down the shaft with such audacious force!

"Pull him up." She commanded.

Everyone found themselves caught up in a shared sense of urgency and determination as they worked tirelessly to pull Slater up the treacherous shaft. Each person exerted every ounce of strength they could muster, their muscles straining against the weight of their collective effort. The atmosphere was electric with tension, each heartbeat echoing like a drum in their ears. Meanwhile, the Bennetts remained steadfastly focused on maintaining their grip on the rope, their hands white-knuckled and resolute. Their unwavering concentration was crucial; they understood that even a momentary lapse could have dire consequences in this precarious situation. As Slater's figure gradually ascended to safety, it became clear that this moment required not just physical strength, but also an unbreakable bond of teamwork and trust among everyone involved.

"So, Slater, as you can see, I'm in no mood to mess around. But would you like some water or a tissue?"

McMatters looked at Jarvis who was struggling to keep his composure as he suppressed laughter. Slater was on the floor, right on the edge of the lift's open shaft.

Santos

Santos and Jarvis's team tried to make it seem like they had lost the ones in Slater's car. After three hours of going around in circles, in and out of town, Jarvis's team called in another team for help. Team two then took the lead in a different car, hoping to convince Slater's team that they had lost their followers. From a considerable distance, they observed the Slater's car, which had suddenly come to a halt. A woman emerged from a house and was stopped by Slater's car, but her identity remained unknown from that far away. It was unsettling to witness the unfolding scene, as the woman appeared to resist fiercely against her captors. They tried to get

228

there to help, but a Police car had just turned the corner, and they did not want the attention of the Police. Despite her struggle and attempts to escape, the woman was ultimately overpowered. The troubling sight became even more alarming when they saw her being forcefully bundled into the boot of the car.

They put their foot down, racing towards the scene of the incident, driven by a mix of urgency and dread. As they sped along, their hearts pounded in sync with the rhythm of the engine, each second feeling like an eternity. They searched frantically for the car involved in the grab, but no trace of it could be found. A sinking realization washed over them; it was clear that the vehicle was no longer on the road. The stretch of road ahead lay empty and desolate, with only echoes of what had just transpired lingering in the air. With a sense of foreboding settling in, they decided to split up into three separate vehicles, each taking a different route to increase their chances of locating any signs or remnants left behind.

Their minds raced with possibilities, as they manoeuvred through unfamiliar terrain, a tangled web of trees lining either side of narrow paths, could easily hide something significant from view. This was more than just a search; it was a race against time. It was tinged with anxiety and uncertainty about what they might discover, as they scoured every inch in pursuit of answers, that seemed increasingly elusive. Santos got on the phone.

"Jarvis, we have an issue. The car, it's vanished! They kidnapped a woman. From the distance, I couldn't tell who it was, we have three cars out searching, but it looks like they are off the road and held up in a building on this stretch."

"Get my guys to get the others out to help."

"Okay, I'll update you soon."

Lorraine

Jarvis leaned in closely, his voice barely above a whisper, as he confided in McMatters, who was visibly worried and deep in thought. The atmosphere was thick with tension; McMatters' brow furrowed as he processed the weight of Jarvis's words. Then, turning his attention to Lorraine, Jarvis delivered the same message with a sense of urgency. The moment she absorbed the information, an unmistakable transformation occurred, a fierce expression of pure anger erupted across her face. It was a powerful reaction that spoke volumes about her feelings on the matter at hand; her eyes blazed with intensity, reflecting not only frustration, but also a readiness to confront Slater.

"Okay, that's it. Down the hole you go, Slater. You see, I don't need you anymore. Untie his arms, but keep his legs tied up for now." Lorraine stood at his feet. "Any last words that might save your arse, Slater?"

Slater laughed heartily, his mirth echoing in the confined space, until he felt Lorraine's firm push against his feet, an unsettling force, that was inexorably nudging him closer to the gaping hole in the lift shaft. "I'm waiting Slater." Lorraine taunted, a glint of mischief dancing in her eyes as she applied more pressure against him.

In that moment of perilous balance, he could feel his head teetering alarmingly over the edge; his arms instinctively flailed as he fought desperately to prevent himself from plummeting into the abyss below. With a sudden burst of determination, Lorraine pushed harder this time. The force sent shockwaves through Slater's body as he found all his upper torso precariously counterbalanced by his legs, struggling mightily against gravity's relentless pull. Panic surged within him, as he realized how close he was to losing everything, his life hanging by a thread and only his willpower standing between him and a catastrophic fall.

"Okay! We will have it your way Slater!"

Meanwhile, the Bennetts quickly sprang into action; they braced themselves with a sturdy rope. A lifeline that would either secure Slater's safety or witness his impending doom. In an instant that passed in slow motion, Slater succumbed to gravity's harsh embrace and fell screaming into the void. Below a chilling sound reverberated off the walls of the dimly lit shaft, as it echoed around them like a haunting refrain of desperation and regret.

"You tell me when you're ready to talk Slater, and we'll pull you up. Oh, I can wait all day, but you can't with all that blood gushing from the cuts on your face. You'll bleed out first."

Within ten minutes, he felt an overwhelming urge to talk, but the reality was that he simply couldn't keep up his resistance any longer. The blood loss was substantial, and each pulse seemed to echo in his ears like a relentless drumbeat, a stark reminder of the life force that was slipping away from him. He could feel the throbbing sensation as his vital fluids drained from his body, leaving him weaker by the second. The pressure in his veins diminished, and with every heartbeat, he realized just how precarious his situation had become. The urgency of his need to communicate, clashed violently with the undeniable truth of his fading strength, creating a desperate struggle within him, as he fought against the encroaching darkness that threatened to engulf him completely.

Chapter Thirty-eight

Searching

Jarvis's teams were deployed in a strategic formation, with three team members in each team, totalling twelve-foot soldiers, methodically canvassing the area where Slater's car had mysteriously vanished. Their careful spread across the terrain underscored the urgency of their task; every shadow and alleyway held potential clues, that could unravel this puzzling disappearance. Meanwhile, the remaining sixteen team members were not idly waiting for information to come to them. Instead, they were actively driving around in different directions, each taking a distinct route through the winding streets and byways of the neighbourhood, desperately seeking any sign or lead that might indicate where Slater's vehicle had gone.

 This multifaceted approach highlighted both the chaos of the situation, and Jarvis's determination to uncover answers amidst ambiguity, revealing an underlying tension as time continued to slip away without resolution. Santos had two teams actively engaged on the ground, working diligently to locate any signs of Slater's car. The inclusion of an additional eight personnel for the search effort, while seemingly minimal, was certainly better than having no extra resources at all. In an unpredictable situation like this, every pair of eyes counts.

Furthermore, Santos had deployed his vehicle alongside one other, extending their search radius slightly further afield. This strategic decision was made, with the cautious assumption that Slater's car might have ventured beyond the initial estimates and expectations of its whereabouts. It demonstrates a critical awareness of the situation's complexity However, it also raises questions about whether these efforts were sufficient in scale and coordination, given the potential risks involved in a broader search operation. They had to stay in a building, waiting for dark when they could slip out of sight more easily.

Chapter Thirty-nine

The Shopping Mall

Jarvis, feeling a sense of urgency and responsibility, made the decision that it was imperative for everyone to participate in the search. He understood that the more individuals they had out scouring the area, the greater their chances would be of locating Katrina, the woman kidnapped by Slater's men, and Blythe's sister. This was not just any search; it was deeply personal for Jarvis, as he held a fondness for Katrina, that added an emotional weight to his commitment. While he enlisted others in this crucial effort, Jarvis resolved to confront Slater directly, alongside McMatters and Lorraine. By taking on Slater himself, he sought not only to address whatever threats or obstacles might arise, but also hoped to ensure that his feelings for Katrina, would not lead him astray during this critical time. The stakes were high; every moment counted in their race against time to find her and bring her back safely.

"Everyone out. Join the search, call in everyone, go find her!"

Slater was laughing, a sound that echoed through the tense atmosphere, which was far from ideal given the precarious situation unfolding around him. The laughter felt almost jarring against the backdrop of urgency, especially since no one was holding the rope anymore, leaving everyone vulnerable and exposed. In a sudden burst of action fuelled by frustration and determination, McMatters delivered a swift punch to Slater's jaw, sending him crashing to the ground in a flurry of surprise and disbelief. As Slater lay there momentarily stunned, McMatters seized the opportunity to undo his ropes with quick efficiency. The air crackled with unspoken understanding, as Lorraine and Jarvis joined in this act of liberation. Their eyes met briefly, each nodding to one another in silent accord, a code that they had all come to recognize without needing words. It was an instinctive acknowledgment of their shared resolve and purpose; they were united in their mission, ready to face whatever challenges lay ahead together.

This bond forged among them might have been born from necessity, but it had blossomed into something deeper: a mutual trust that transcended spoken language and solidified their alliance amidst chaos.

In the dimly lit room, a palpable tension hung in the air as everyone understood that Slater would remain silent. He would never divulge the details of his actions or reveal the whereabouts of Blythe's sister. The weight of this unspoken truth loomed over them, heavy and oppressive. One by one, they took turns delivering their blows, kicking and punching Slater with a ferocity born from anger and desperation. It was a calculated release, an expression of their frustration and pain, directed at this elusive figure who held so many secrets. As Lorraine and McMatters stepped back to allow Jarvis his moment, the atmosphere shifted; it became charged with anticipation.

This was Jarvis's turn, the culmination of their collective rage poised to erupt in one decisive act. With fierce determination, he lunged forward and delivered one fatal blow that connected solidly with Slater's body, sending him reeling backwards. Slater staggered precariously on the edge of the lift shaft, desperately searching for something, anything to grasp onto as he teetered on the brink of disaster. His fingers clawed at the thin air, in a futile attempt to regain his balance; however, no support awaited him in that void. In an instant that felt like an eternity, Slater succumbed to gravity's unforgiving pull and fell down the dark shaft below. The sound of his body hitting the bottom resonated through them all like a haunting echo sharp and jarring a grim reminder of their actions as it reverberated off the walls of their shared reality. It pierced through their collective consciousness, leaving behind a chilling silence filled only by their racing hearts and heavy breaths.

Dreams Collection continues in book three with Living.

With the clock ticking in the urgent race to locate Katrine, hope hangs delicately in the balance...will they succeed in saving her? As new intelligence emerges, it brings with it revelations that could change everything and lead to drastic consequences for everyone involved. In this tense atmosphere, relationships will be put to the ultimate test; loyalties will be questioned, and bonds strained under pressure. Will Maxine manage to navigate through this chaos and emerge unscathed? One must wonder: amidst such turmoil and uncertainty, can love truly endure against all odds? This harrowing journey beckons not just for survival but for a reaffirmation of the strength of human connection when faced with unimaginable challenges.

Living

Coming Soon!

Joanne
Keele

Printed in Great Britain
by Amazon